Edge of the Badlands

LANCE HAYDEN

A Black Horse Western

ROBERT HALE · LONDON

Robert Hale Limited
Clerkenwell House
Clerkenwell Green
London EC1R 0HT

Typeset by
Derek Doyle & Associates, Liverpool.
Printed and bound in Great Britain by
Antony Rowe Limited, Wiltshire

1

Ghost Town

The red ball of the prairie sun was still an hour above the canebrake to the west of the trail when Neil Vance took a last drink from his canteen and leaned forward, resting his arms on the pommel of the saddle. Hills rose to the north and seemed to swell up around the wide sweep of the horizon where the trail unwound along the northern bank of the wide river, flanked on either side by the flowing grass of the prairie. He ran his gaze swiftly over the trail as he sat still in the saddle. This was still wild and untamed country and he had known for a long time that there was danger waiting for him somewhere along the trail. But if he felt a little apprehensive about what lay in front of him, none of it showed through on his bluff, clear-cut features. He had a job to do, and he intended to do it.

Sliding the canteen back into its pouch, he put his spurs gently to the stallion, urging it forward. Ten miles or so to the north-west lay the town of Big Wheel and it was his intention to reach it before nightfall. A small place from what little he knew of it, but nevertheless, it boasted one hotel and six gambling saloons, all of which were owned by the same man, a crooked shyster named Clint McCord. But Vance's business was not with this man. The frontier towns were full of gamblers and tin-horn crooks like McCord; and no doubt the law would get around to cleaning these places up once it had dealt with the bigger crooks; the killers and stage robbers who had a price on their heads.

As he rode, sitting tall and easy in the saddle, his guns worn low, he kept a quick eye on the trees that rose up black on the side of thé trail half a mile ahead. He was a tall man for that country, slimly-built, but with a wiry strength which showed itself in the corded muscles of his arms and the restless eyes which were hard and blue, like chips of ice. The horse under him was a long, leggy animal that had plenty of strength and wind and was definitely suited to the wild country which lay ahead of him. Beneath the blue shirt, hidden where no one would be able to spot it until the right time, was the star of a Texas Marshal. He was the last of four to enter this territory and then pass through Big Wheel, heading southward along the old pioneer trail into the Badlands which stretched clear to the border with New Mexico.

Neil Vance was thinking of this as he rode along the river trail on the last mile or so to his initial destination. He knew that it was possible he would meet the same fate as those three men, but it was this thought which, more than anything else, had spurred him on during the long, hard ride across the prairie country to the east.

He had been in Dodge when word had come through that Clem Hagberg, one of the most vicious killers the west had ever known, had been located in the Badlands which lay to the south of Big Wheel. Then, it had meant little to him. Other men had been assigned to the task of flushing out the killer and any others he may have drawn to him, and bringing him back to justice. But three Rangers had gone into that country after Hagberg and none of them had returned. Their fate was still a matter of conjecture, and would likely have remained a complete mystery had not Bart Payson's mount made it back to Big Wheel two days after he had vanished; and there had been blood on the saddle which told its own ominous story.

It had taken him eight days from Dodge and as he had ridden westwards, the character of the country had changed enormously. He had left the smooth, level plains behind and entered a wild country of tall, rolling hills and wide rivers, craggy ridges lined with hackberry bushes and thorn; a country which, without doubt, was one of the best for hiding out from the law. The blue-clad cavalry had ridden through this way a couple of years back and had even got to the point of establishing a military fort some twenty miles along the river, but they were seriously under-manned and unable to field any punitive forces into the Badlands. For the most part, they left this stretch of country alone, left it to the killers, the marauding bands of men who had deserted from the South during the time of the Civil War, who had never settled down to the new life after one of killing and slaughtering, of plunder and pillage, and who had gone their own way, keeping one step ahead of the law.

Such a man was Clem Hagberg. Vance ran over in his mind all that he had learned about this man, back in Dodge. Once a Lieutenant with the South, he had been drummed out of the Confederate Army for cowardice in the face of the enemy and following on the defeat of the Confederacy, he had turned killer and bank robber. The price on his head was ten thousand dollars, dead or alive. And added to that, thought Vance grimly, was the almost undeniable fact that he had killed the three Rangers who had gone into the Badlands after him.

The sun went down behind the canebrake as he topped the low rise and set his horse at the downward loop of the trail. Like all good lawmen, he rode with his eyes and ears wide open and when he was within half a mile of Big Wheel, he heard the unmistakable sound of gunfire. Instantly on the alert, he set his heels to the stallion's flanks, urging it into a gallop. There was no sign of any smoke up ahead and he told himself that he might be wrong altogether, and this was nothing more than a group of ranch-hands giving vent to their feelings by loosing off a few shots in the streets of Big Wheel.

When he rode into the wide, dusty street a few minutes later, everything was quiet. He halted his mount at the end of the street and sat quite still in the saddle, hands resting on the guns in their leather holsters, eyes flicking from side to side, ready to pick out the slightest movement. But nothing moved and all sound had faded as he had approached the town. Very slowly, he rode forward, easing the guns from their holsters now, holding them carefully in his hands, growing more and more worried with every passing second. Where was everyone? As far as he had been able to make out, Big Wheel, although not a large frontier town, had a population of close on three hundred. Now, it was as if every one of them – every man, woman, and child – had been spirited away into the darkness, leaving behind a ghost town in which nothing lived or moved.

The little germ of apprehension began to grow in the pit of his stomach. On one side of the street, he made out the saloon. There was a faint light showing in one of the wide windows and acting on impulse, he reined his horse and slid cautiously from the saddle, hitching it over the rail, before going forward, moving cat-like and silent on to the boardwalk. Very gently, he pushed open the batwing doors and stepped inside. The light came from a single lamp over the bar. Reflected from the wide glass mirror at the back, it lit the room with a pale, diffuse glow. Several of the tables had been knocked over and here and there a chair lay smashed into splinters. But apart from that, the place was empty.

Slowly, he made his way up the wide stairway, paused at the top, facing the long corridor in front of him. The doors on either side were all closed. He went into the rooms one by one. All were empty. In one of them, a small mirror had been shattered by a bullet and a couple of chairs were overturned. Going back down the stairs, he paused instinctively at the bottom as the faint sound reached his ears. Without hesitating, he dived in behind the bar, came up behind the man who lay there and pushed the muzzle of his Colt hard in the small of the man's back. This time, in a situation like this, he was taking no chances.

'All right, mister,' he said tightly. 'Just turn around nice and easy and let me take a good look at yuh.'

'Don't shoot, I ain't armed.' Vance noticed with surprise, that the other was shivering violently. The man turned his head slowly and stared at him with wide, frightened eyes, then a curious look crept over the bearded face and the eyes slowly narrowed. 'Say, you ain't one o' them.' The man backed up against the bar, glanced down at the gun in Vance's hand, then wet his lips.

'When did you ride into town, mister?'

'Five minutes ago,' replied Vance. But I'll ask the questions. Where is everybody? The town is as dead as a morgue. I thought I heard shooting too, as I rode in.'

'You heard shootin' all right, mister.' The other cackled harshly and Vance realized that he was half drunk. He would have to work fast if he was to get any sense out of this old coot before he passed out altogether.

'Then who was it? And where are all the others who ought to be in town right now?'

The drunk leaned forward and Vance felt his nose wrinkle as the man's breath assailed his nostrils. 'Mister, I don't know where you just come from: and I don't know which way yuh trail is headed, but if you take the advice of Cal Brown, you'll get on your horse and ride straight outa Big Wheel and never come back.'

'Any real reason why I should do that?' muttered Vance thinly. He holstered the gun as he realized that Brown was unarmed and there was no menace from him anyway.

'Could be you've never heard tell of Clem Hagberg.

Otherwise yuh wouldn't be waiting around to git a bullet in your belly.'

Vance tightened his lips. He had half expected this, but here was the proof he needed. 'Hagberg! Sure, I've heard of him. One of the renegades from the war, a killer. I heard he might be hiding out in these parts but I wasn't sure. So he's behind all this.'

'That's right, mister. When you git word that Hagberg and his bunch are due to hit town, yuh just pack up and leave until it's all over.'

Vance stared at the old-timer in surprise. 'You mean that everybody just upped and left?'

'That's right. They'll come straggling back tomorrow or the next day, when they figure it's safe to come. Apart from the two of us, the whole town is probably deserted.'

'Meanwhile, you decided to stay behind and help yourself to some free liquor. Probably figgered Hagberg would not bother shooting a rat like you.'

Brown merely shrugged and sagged against the bar. His eyes were glazing over and Vance guessed that he would get little more information out of him before he passed out completely. 'I ain't no friend of Hagberg's,' muttered Brown, moistening his lips. His voice was suddenly slurred and Vance felt his deadweight drag on his arm. He curled his lips in disgust and let the other go. The man slumped forward, bending at the knees, then collapsed into a drunken heap in front of him. Stepping over him, Vance made his way to the doors and pushed through them into the street. It was almost dark now and a few stars lit the sky overhead. Leading his horse, he made his way slowly along the main street, eyes and ears alert, but there was no sign of any life and by the time he reached the far side of town, he knew that the old man in the saloon had been right. The place was a ghost town, empty, all of the citizens fleeing from the fury of Clem Hagberg and his band of killers.

There was no sense in riding further that night. To go out into the Badlands in total darkness would be asking for trouble. Besides, he had ridden long and hard for the past eight days and this might be the last chance he would get to rest up awhile. He knew that he could ignore the presence of the old-timer in the saloon down the street. Cal Brown would be out for the rest of the night and there seemed little chance of Hagberg and his men returning that night. They had been in the town already, knew that it was deserted, and any loot or vittles they had wanted they would have taken before they left. By now, he figured that they would be quite a distance to the south, heading for their hideout somewhere in the Badlands.

There was also the chance that someone in Big Wheel might know something about Hagberg and his band, and also of what had happened to the three Rangers who had ridden south to bring him in and who had undoubtedly been killed.

He located the livery stable in an open lot near the centre of the town and pushed open the creaking door. Everything was in darkness inside, but he found a lantern and lit it, placing it on one of the stalls. There was plenty of fodder around and he led his mount into one of the stables, making sure that it was watered and that there was plenty of food for it. The hotel was just across the street from the stables and his boots made a hollow sound as he walked up the wooden steps and went inside. The sound of his footsteps seemed to emphasize the eerie emptiness of the town. At the back of the hotel he found some tins of beans and bacon and cooked himself a meal over the fire which he lit in the big kitchen. It seemed strange walking into a place like this and taking everything for the asking. When the inhabitants of Big Wheel returned the next day, he would pay for what he had taken, but in the meantime, he realized just how hungry he really was. When he had eaten his fill, he made his way up the narrow straight stairs and entered the first bedroom he could find.

He woke early the next morning to the sound of horses'

hoofbeats in the street outside the window. Swiftly, fully alert, he swung his legs to the floor and padded over to the window. A couple of wagons were coming along the main street and behind them came a group of men on horse-back. It was time he got up and showed himself, he decided.

Ten minutes later, when he left the room and walked slowly down the stairs, he heard the sound of someone moving around in the room below and as he reached the bottom, a tall man, standing in the middle of the long hall-way, suddenly glanced up, saw him standing there and went for his gun. Vance made no move towards his.

'Jest keep them paws in sight or I'll plug yuh,' grated the other thinly. Without turning his head, he yelled 'Hey Clark. See what I've got here.'

Out of the corner of his eye, flicking his gaze over the other's shoulder, Vance saw the short, wiry figure of the second man come into view. The heavily-jowled features expressed surprise, then a cunning suspicion. He said thickly: 'Where'd you spring from, cowboy?'

Vance jerked his thumb in the direction of the stairs. 'Rode in last night,' he said easily, keeping one eye on the *hombre* with the gun. There was a strained look on the other's white face and Vance guessed that he was an inex-perienced man with a gun. Such a man was liable to press the trigger at the slightest move, to plug a man and ask questions afterwards. He had still been sleepy when he had walked down the stairs, but now his head cleared fast.

'Yuh say you rode in last night?' The short man's lips curled in a faintly sneering grin. 'I'll say yuh did. Rode in with Hagberg and figgered that you'd git yourself a free bed for the night. Well, I've got news fer yuh, cowboy. Yuh friends left during the night and you're all alone right now.'

Vance grew wooden, keeping a careful watch on the man with the gun. 'You've got this figgered all wrong,' he said quietly, keeping his hands in front of him. 'I rode in from the east just before dark last night. Been on the trail for close on nine days, all the way from Dodge. Heard shooting on my way in and took it easy, didn't want to git mixed up in any gunplay until I knew what it was all about. When I got here, found the place deserted except for an old guy in the saloon along the street. Tried to get some sense outa him, but all he could tell me was that everybody had left because of this killer Hagberg. Then he passed out cold on me. You'll find him back there if you care to check on my story. He'll tell yuh, if he can remember anything.'

'Don't you worry, mister, we'll check,' muttered the other. He turned to the tall man. 'Jest keep him covered while I git the Sheriff. Once this *hombre* is in jail, we can soon find out if he's telling the truth.'

After the other had gone, Vance leaned back against the rail and regarded the other from unwinking eyes, holding him, able to read him if he should move into action. He knew that even if he went for his gun, he could shoot this man down before he could make a move, but he had never shot an innocent man in his life before, even to get himself out of a jam like this. Besides, if he could have a heart-to-heart talk with the sheriff of this town, he might be able to learn more than by questioning any of the townsfolk who seemed to have a tendency to shut up like clams when questioned.

The stockily-built man came back a few minutes later, accompanied by the tall, thin-faced man with the Sheriff's badge on his shirt. He looked Neil Vance over speculatively, eyes narrowed, but there was no recognition in his gaze and finally, he shook his head. 'Don't recognize this fella,' he said harshly. 'But that don't mean to say he isn't with that bunch of killers. Reckon you'd better bring him along to the office, Hank. Keep that gun on him, just in case. He looks as though he could use them irons of his.'

'Want me to take 'em, jest in case?' asked the man called Clark.

'Reckon you'd better,' agreed the sheriff finally. 'We'll all feel a mite safer if you do.'

There was nothing that Vance could do. The short man came forward, taking good care not to step into the line of fire of his companion's gun and slid his guns out of their holsters. A few moments later, Vance was prodded along the boardwalk towards the sheriff's office.

Seating himself behind the desk, the other looked at him hard, eyes narrowed. The two men stood in the background of the office, their eyes never leaving him.

'Now stranger. Perhaps you'd like to tell us jest who yuh are and where you're from.'

Vance shrugged. 'That's easy explained, Sheriff,' he said smoothly. 'But I'd prefer to talk in private. The fewer people know my business in these parts, the better.'

The sheriff's eyes narrowed just a shade. He looked Vance up and down appraisingly. 'You figger me fer a fool?' he grated finally.

'Now what could I do, Sheriff?' argued Vance. 'Your henchmen have got my guns and you're armed.'

The other paused, then gave a brief nod. 'Wait outside, men,' he said tersely. 'If I yell, come running.'

The men nodded. stepped out on to the boardwalk, closing the door behind them. Vance relaxed There were probably guns trained on him from outside at that very moment, but he ignored that possibility. Reaching inside his shirt, he pulled off the Marshal's badge of office and tossed it on to the other's desk. It lay on the polished wood, glinting brilliantly in the rays of the sun which streamed in through the solitary window. The sheriff eyed it for a moment in surprise, then picked it up and held it in his fingers for a long moment before lifting his head and looking hard at Vance.

'A Texas Marshal,' he said thinly. The suspicion was still there at the back of his eyes, but there was a note of new respect in his tone. Finally, he leaned back in his chair and gave a slow nod. 'I figgered they might send another man out here sometime, but you could have fooled me. Yuh look like a killer, I must admit, from the way you wore your guns. You aiming to go into the Badlands after the Hagberg gang?'

'Perhaps,' grunted Vance non-committally. He picked up the badge from the desk and slipped it inside his shirt again. 'Now you see why I didn't want those two men in the room. Three Rangers have been killed going after Hagberg and I don't figger on becoming the fourth victim. Word can easily filter out to Hagberg that I'm in town and just what my business is. The fewer people know why I'm here and who I am, the better. Seems to me that those three men who went after him before, trusted somebody in Big Wheel who's in league with these killers. Those men knew their job. They'd have made a fight of it if they'd been given an even shake. I don't reckon they got that. I figger they were gunned down before they knew what was happening, by somebody who knew who they were beforehand.'

'You got any ideas where Hagberg might be hiding out?'

'Nope. But this is as good a place to start looking.'

'In Big Wheel.' The other's brows lifted in surprise. 'Say, you don't reckon they're still here, do yuh?' There was a trace of fear in the sheriff's voice which did not go unnoticed by Vance.

He shook his head. 'Not exactly. But I figger that somebody in town knows where their hideout is. Last reports I got, a couple of stages had been held up two miles out of here. Both times, they got away with gold bullion. They must have been tipped off about that.'

'So you figger there's somebody hereabouts giving them information,' mused the other. 'Could be. Suspected one or two men myself but I've never bin able to pin anything on 'em.'

'Any objections if I look around the town myself in the next couple of days? I'd like to know what I'm heading into before I light out into the desert.'

'Sure, help yourself,' agreed the other affably. 'Don't reckon you'll find out much in two days though. I've been trying myself for close on three months, even before those three Rangers showed up here. Reckon I'd have stood a better chance than you. Still, if you want to ask a few questions around Big Wheel, that's your affair. And I'll keep your identity a secret.'

'Thanks, Sheriff.' Vance straightened up and chuckled as he replied: 'If I do find that dirty rattler who's been tipping Hagberg off, I aim to kill him myself. Save you the trouble of getting a rope and hanging him.'

If the other was surprised by the deep intensity in the Marshal's tone, he gave no outward sign. He got slowly to his feet, balancing his weight on his knuckles on top of the desk. 'Need any help at all, Marshal?'

Vance shook his head. 'Not until I locate Hagberg's hideout in the Badlands. Then I may need a posse to back me up when I go in after him.'

'Just say the word and I'll come along myself. Been wanting to catch this killer myself, but he's too smart and slippery.'

Vance narrowed his eyes a little. The thought came to him that if the Sheriff had been so anxious to catch up with Hagberg and his band, he had only to stay in town when the raiders put in an appearance and he would have got as many chances as he wanted. But that was a thought best kept to himself until he knew how much he could rely on the other to help him. At the moment, he trusted no one. Those two men still standing outside the door with drawn guns had been just a mite too anxious to pick him up as one of the Hagberg gang. The more he reflected on it, the more logical it seemed that it would have been as good a way as any of getting him out of the way. A quick lynching party by enraged citizens and that would have been the end of Marshal Neil Vance.

'What do I tell those two hombres outside the door when they see me walk out of here?' he asked humorously.

'I'll explain things to them so that they don't get too curious,' said the other tightly. 'You've got to remember that everybody is a mite edgy now. Those killers took everything they needed when they hit town yesterday and they never paid a cent for it.'

'Then why don't you fight, instead of running away like mice? There must be enough good men in Big Wheel who can handle a gun. Why run away when you can stay right here and defend what rightfully belongs to you. Surely that would be the best way to deal with killers like these; in fact it's the only way.'

The other nodded slowly. 'That's true, Marshal. But we all know what Hagberg and his hired gunslingers are like. There isn't a single family in town who hasn't suffered in some way or other at their hands. They won't stand up to these men and Hagberg knows it. That's how he's managed to terrorize the entire territory.'

'Perhaps we may be able to alter that in the future,' said Vance grimly. 'In the meantime, I'll book in at the hotel legal like this time, then start asking a few questions. In particular, I want to know who were the last people to see either of those three Rangers before they went out into the Badlands. And also who found that horse with the blood on the saddle, the one that came back.'

The sheriff thought for a minute, then nodded: 'If I remember rightly, it was Marty Benson who found that mount. He's one of the old prospectors who comes into town on odd occasions. If he is here, you'll usually find him in the Golden Nugget saloon. You can't mistake him.'

'Thanks. I'll look him up. Just one thing more, Sheriff. The nearest Army depot is about fifty miles away to the north, I understand. Do you ever get them riding into this area?'

Surprise was written over the other's face at the sudden

question, then he caught himself and shrugged briefly: 'They sometimes come into town when on patrol but that isn't very often. Any particular reason for asking, Marshal?'

'No, just wondering how far away they might be if we needed troops in a hurry. Judging by the way in which the people of this town act, that gang of Hagberg's must be a pretty big one. Could be that your posse might not be big enough to deal with them when the time comes.'

The sheriff bridled a little at the suggestion and said quickly: 'Once I swear in a posse, Marshal, they'll follow me to the end of the west, even into the Badlands if I give the order.'

'I hope you're right.' Vance nodded and made for the door. 'When the time of reckoning comes, I'll need every man I can get, provided he can handle a gun.'

Cranwell Morgan, who ran most things in Big Wheel, according to the bartender in the Golden Nugget saloon, stood with his back to Vance and stared out of the window into the dry, dusty street that shimmered in the heat of the noon sun. His thick, fleshy jaws were clamped tightly around a long cigar and his every look exuded prosperity. But Vance wasn't fooled none. He had found out a little about this man during the past hour and by careful questioning on his contacts among the ordinary folk of the town, he knew that Morgan was not only a clever card-sharp and gambler, but that he had an unsavoury background. There was talk of murder, but no actual proof of that; and no names were mentioned. He might, or he might not, be in league with Hagberg. That was something Vance wanted to find out before he went much further. But all in all, it seemed doubtful that the other could have reached his present status without some shady deals and a handful of hired killers to back him.

Finally, the other turned and surveyed Vance with pale eyes. 'I must confess that you interest me,' he said quietly, keeping the cigar firmly fixed between his thick lips. 'But I still can't figure why you came to see me.' He moved across the room and lowered his huge bulk into the chair at the back of the ornate, polished, mahogany desk and toyed with the slender-bladed knife which lay on top of it. 'You say that Sheriff Torlin told you to come here. That I find hard to believe. The Sheriff does exactly as I tell him and I did not ask for you to be sent to see me. Nevertheless, I do like to know what is happening in town.' His vulture stare went over Vance from head to toe, not pausing once but taking in everything. 'You look like a man who can handle a gun,' he said finally, abruptly. 'Looking for a job?'

'Could be,' agreed Vance non-committally. 'I ain't got any roots anywhere, and a guy has to eat, I reckon. As you say, I can handle this gun if I have to.'

'When I hire a man to do something, I like to consider it done. You understand that, don't you?'

'Shore.' Vance hunched his shoulders. 'Only just what is it you've got in mind – murder?'

Morgan's brows shot up. 'You talk like a fool,' he said testily, biting the end off a fresh cigar. He pulled out a match, struck it and touched it to the end of the cigar, blowing a cloud of smoke in front of him. Through this haze, he eyed Vance shrewdly. 'Just where are you from, cowboy?' He placed the spent match carefully in a small silver tray. 'Back east, you told the Sheriff. I'd like it a little more precise than that.'

'Dodge,' said Vance briefly. There was no point in lying at this stage. The other might have ways and means of checking on his story and Dodge City was far enough away to enable him to use his own name. The one disturbing thought was that if the Sheriff was in Morgan's pay, he might spill the news as to his identity and that would mean he would have to come out into the open long before he was ready to do so.

'Know anything about a man who calls himself Clem

Hagberg?' Morgan leaned back in his chair, removed the cigar from his lips and ran it gently over his mouth. The pale eyes never left Vance's face.

'Hagberg? Sure, who hasn't? A renegade from the War, hiding somewhere out in the Badlands south of Big Wheel. He came into the town last night. That's why I found a ghost town when I rode in. Seems to me everybody in these parts is scared to death of him. Must be a pretty big man.'

Morgan then said gently: 'He may be a big man as far as the townsfolk are concerned, but to me, he's just another killer and I want him out of the way. You'll know by now that I own this town, lock, stock and barrel. All of the property that you can see belongs to me. Most of the prairie around Big Wheel is also mine, all filed legally and well documented. So you see why I can't have Hagberg riding roughshod through this territory much longer. There are several gold veins in the hills to the north. I get a percentage on everything found there by the prospectors. They also spend their money in the saloons, so indirectly everything comes back to me. But if Hagberg continues to raid the town whenever he feels like it, then business is going to decline as far as I'm concerned.'

The slate-coloured, frosty eyes bored into Vance's. 'I want Hagberg killed and I want it fast. I don't care how it's done, just so long as he doesn't get under my hide another day. Understand?'

'That ain't going to be so easy.' Vance thought fast. This was something he hadn't been expecting. He had come here with the express purpose of hunting down Clem Hagberg and his gang of killers and now this man was offering him the job of doing exactly that. Admittedly the reasons were very different but it still seemed faintly ironic.

'If you reckon you can't handle it, just say so, and I'll find myself a man who can.'

Vance thought fast. This was certainly a novel way of

hunting down a killer gang; and it also had plenty of possibilities. If he agreed to go in with Morgan, he would be acting with the most powerful man in Big Wheel and there was a far better chance of learning some useful information than trying to work on his own. Morgan knew something about the slaying of those three Rangers, Vance felt sure of that.

'I'll handle it,' he said shortly. 'But I'd like to know exactly where I stand. You'll have your own men in on this deal too, I reckon. I don't want to take orders from any of them. I work best alone.'

'I figured you would,' said the other easily, unperturbed. He lowered the cigar and flicked the grey ash off the end into the tray. 'Makes no difference, though.' He began talking in a strangely mollifying tone of voice. 'I've got thirty men on my payroll. Some are owners of the hotels and saloons in town. They take their orders from me, though. I don't like everybody to know that I run the place. You'll be on the same footing as everybody else who works for me. But if you want to work the lone wolf, that's okay by me, so long as it pays results. You booked up at the hotel?'

Vance nodded. 'That's right. Got me a room as soon as I left the sheriff's office. Figured on staying here for a little while. Never thought I'd have a job offered to me.'

The pale eyes never wavered. 'That job's open only so long as you rate it,' said the flat, emotionless voice. 'Figure I ought to warn you that some of the men mightn't like another hombre on the payroll. You ain't met Matt Devlin yet?'

'Haven't had that pleasure,' said Vance slowly.

'You will.' His eyes flickered down to the gunbelt around the other's waist. 'He reckons he's the fastest draw this side of the Mississippi. I've never seen him matched against Hagberg. I might see him against you, though.'

'Any reason why I should draw on him?' asked Vance curiously.

The pale brows lifted a fraction. 'Could be that he's a jealous *hombre*. That's one of the reasons I hired him.'

'That suits me,' muttered Vance thinly. 'I don't aim to cause any trouble with this hombre, but if he wants it, he'll get it.'

The noon sun blazed down on the main street of Big Wheel as Vance stepped out of the saloon and walked across to the hotel. His horse had been fed and watered at the livery stable and around him, life seemed to be returning to normal in the town. Little eddies of yellow dust chased themselves along the street in front of the faint breeze that blew right off the desert to the south and held no refreshing coolness in it. He had inquired in the saloon about Marty Benson, the old prospector who had found the Ranger's horse as it had returned from the Badlands. But he had not been seen there for close on five weeks and no one knew where he was, nor when he was likely to return. All that he learned was that if the old-timer stuck to his usual habits, he ought to hit town within the next day or so.

As he reached the door of his room, some sixth sense warned him that someone stood on the other side of it. Gently, he eased one of the sixguns from its holster and twisted the handle of the door. It turned easily and with a sudden jerk, he thrust it open and stepped into the room, the gun ready in his right hand. Then he pulled up short, lowering the gun.

The girl, seated in the chair by the window, was watching him with a faintly amused expression in her eyes. For a moment, Vance stared at her, feeling suddenly foolish, then thrust the gun back into its holster. Now that he had time for a closer look, he saw that she was tall for a woman, almost as tall as he himself, and her dark, flashing eyes watching him closely from beneath a smooth brow. She was part Spanish ancestry, he reflected, no doubt about that, and there seemed to be a slightly cruel streak in the set of her mouth.

'Sorry I pulled that gun on you, Ma'am,' he said quietly. 'Fact is, I wasn't expecting any visitors, and when I heard someone moving around in my room, I decided to take no chances. From what I've seen and heard, this place can be mighty unhealthy if a man isn't cautious.'

'I hear you've been talking with my father,' she said in a quiet voice. Then, noticing the look of surprise on his face, went on: 'I'm Carla Morgan. Please sit down, I want to talk to you.'

He lowered himself into the other chair. He wished that Morgan had given him warning of this possibility. He liked her voice, and yet there was a sting to it too, as if she was accustomed to giving orders and anyone who didn't jump to obey them found they had a veritable wildcat by the tail. For the first time, he noticed the whip which lay coiled beside her, within easy reach of her right hand.

'I suppose that my father offered you a job in Big Wheel,' she said smoothly. It was more of a statement than a question. 'Did you accept it?'

'Yes. Figured I might need some employment if I'm to stay here awhile.' Deep inside, his mind was whirling furiously, trying to figure out some reason for this visit, this sudden interest in him.

'I thought you might. You look as though you could be pretty handy with those guns of yours. And I suppose he warned you against Devlin.'

'He did mention the name,' agreed Vance slowly. 'Why? You figuring that I might have trouble with him too?'

He ought to have known from the faint, enigmatic smile on her lips and the cruel light in the dark, flashing eyes, that trouble was not very far away. But the voice behind him was the first indication he had that there was someone else in the room, hiding in the corner. He cursed himself for having walked into such a trap with his eyes open.

'Reckon you've already got trouble with him, stranger.'

He came lithely to his feet, turning swiftly, but making

no move to go for his guns. If the other had his already out, then he stood very little chance of cutting him down. If he still had them holstered, relying on the quickness of his draw, then there might be all the time in the world to make his play.

The man standing in the corner of the room, leaning his back against the wall was short, wiry, with eyes that seemed to lack any colour of their own. They were watching Vance now with the open, unfocused stare of a killer, ready to make his play the instant the other man made a move. Vance grinned. 'So you're Devlin,' he said smoothly. 'I figured we'd meet up with each other sometime, but I never guessed it would be as soon as this.' He watched the girl out of the corner of his vision, but she had not moved from the chair, only her right hand had slid down a little, the strong, slender fingers now gripping the whip tightly. There was an almost expectant look on her face and he saw the tip of her tongue moisten her parted lips. Now Vance knew the reason behind all this. She wanted to see which man proved the quicker on the draw. The cruel streak in her, probably inherited from a fiery mother, was still dominant. He had the vague feeling that she was probably even stronger-willed than her father, that she might be the real brains behind everything that went on in Big Wheel.

Then he flicked his gaze back to Devlin. There was nothing to fear from Carla Morgan yet, he realized. She would wait to see the outcome of this meeting of two men before making her own play, whatever that might be.

'They tell me that you're pretty fast with those guns of yours,' said Vance thinly, watching the other closely. 'I ain't got nothing against you, don't even know you, but if you're so keen on making a play, then I reckon you'd better get it over.'

The other's lips thinned, then twisted back into a sneer. 'No point in shedding blood in front of a lady,' he said sharply, his hands lowering themselves slowly to the buckle

of the gunbelt, loosening it and allowing the guns to drop
to the floor. 'It will be just as easy to take you apart with my
bare hands.'

One glance at the other was enough to tell Vance that
the man would be a dirty fighter. Even before his own
gunbelt was bucking to the floor, the other came rushing
in, aiming a heavy right at Vance's chin. Barely in time,
Vance leaned back, riding the blow on his shoulder. In his
eagerness to punish Vance, the other made the mistake of
rushing in too quickly and for an instant, he was
completely off balance. Seizing his chance, Vance hit him
twice, once to the ribs and then to the side of the face.
Devlin staggered, fell against the wall and hung there for
a moment, sucking air down into his gasping lungs. Vance
eased himself back into the middle of the room, where he
would have more space in which to manoeuvre. Even as he
moved, Devlin came boring in again, feinting with his
right hand, then lashing out with a vicious kick. It caught
Vance on his right side, scraping the flesh. He fell sideways
and instantly, the other threw himself on him, pinning
him to the floor, one hand squeezing tightly around the
lawman's throat, plainly trying to throttle him.

Brutally intent on strangling him, Devlin shifted his
body to add his weight to his arms. Feeling his senses
going, Vance used his legs and shoulders to unseat the
other, heaving him sideways with all the strength he could
muster. The other's hands slid reluctantly from around his
throat and he sucked air thankfully into his lungs.
Gradually, the haze in front of his eyes went away and now
he could feel his strength returning. He thrust himself to
his feet split seconds before the other pushed himself on
to his knees and drove a hard fist into Devlin's face. He felt
flesh and cartilage go as blood spurted from the other's
nose. Devlin let out a bellow of pain and rage, twisted
forward on his knees and brought up both fists into
Vance's chest. Pain seared across his ribs and then everything was forgotten in the fury that seized him. Ignoring

the pain, he drove the other man before him until Devlin was backed against the wall in the corner, hammering at his body with fists that seemed to have no feeling in them. The blood was pounding in his ears and only dimly was he aware of the fact that the other had slid into a sitting position with only the wall holding him up. Stepping back, breathing heavily, he stood staring down at the half-conscious form in front of him. Then he turned to face the girl.

'I reckon you'd both better leave,' he said tightly. 'I don't profess to know your particular motives in this, but I do understand his. So I'm working for your father. Well, he gave me a free hand in this and I need help from no one. If Devlin gets in my way again, he'd better be ready to use his gun, because I'll kill him.'

For a moment, he saw the whiteness in her face and the tight lips compressed into a thin line. She rose lithely to her feet and stared across at him, almost matching him for height. 'No one speaks to me like that,' she flared angrily. 'So you gave Devlin a beating. But you'll find that I can be more dangerous than he is. I know why my father hired you – to kill Clem Hagberg.' Her lips twitched into a thin smile and she toyed with the whip in her hands. 'I don't think you'll find that quite so easy as beating Devlin.'

He saw her gaze flick over his shoulder, saw the sudden look that came into her dark eyes, and whirled swiftly, moving forward savagely as if he had already sensed the danger. Devlin had recovered consciousness and already, he was bending towards the guns lying on the floor. Swiftly, Vance stamped down on the outstretched hand, crushing the fingers with all of his weight. Devlin uttered a loud yell of pain, and recoiled instantly, leaning against the wall. There was the will to murder written plainly in his eyes, his stare bright with malevolence and in the set expression on his face, there was the promise of some future accounting.

Keeping a watchful eye on the other, Vance bent, picked up his own gunbelt and buckled it around his waist. Now, he felt prepared for anything, even a wildcat such as Carla Morgan. Picking up Devlin's belt, he moved the guns from their holsters, shook the bullets from the chambers, then handed the belt back to the other.

'Remember what I said, Devlin,' muttered Vance thinly. 'If you ever try anything like that again, use your gun.'

'Make no mistake about it, *hombre*, I will.' Buckling on his belt, the other strode to the door and pulled it open with a savage gesture. He turned to took at Carla Morgan. For a moment, the girl hesitated, stared closely at Vance, then she walked forward. As she drew level with him, she said softly. 'It's a pity that you said what you did to me. We could have worked well together. I like a man who knows how to take care of himself. But Devlin is anxious to kill you now. Then my father will have to find someone else to go out into the Badlands after Clem Hagberg.'

There was a faint scent, an elusive perfume surrounding her as she swept out of the room. For a moment, Vance stood quite still, then closed the door behind them. He went over to the jug and basin in the corner of the room, poured some of the cold water into the basin and washed his face. The coolness of it took away some of the ache, but there was a bruise on his cheek where the other's fist had grazed along the flesh and it was tender to the touch.

Glancing out of the window, a moment later, he saw Carla Morgan come out into the street and stand in the bright sunlight beside Devlin. They appeared to be arguing together. Then Carla said something which Vance did not hear and Devlin spun sharply on his heel and walked along the street. Outside the saloon, he unhitched a horse from the rail, swung himself up slowly into the saddle and kicked spurs to the mount, riding off out of town along the trail which would take him south,

into the Badlands. As the dust settled, Carla Morgan
walked over to the other side of the street into the sheriff's office.

2

Bushwack Trail

From the window of his room, Vance saw the old prospector ride in from the north, seated on the old burrow, a couple of sacks thrown over the worn saddle, behind him. Vance narrowed his eyes and he took in everything about the other. So this was the man who might be able to help him, he mused. He watched as the other rode slowly to the saloon, slid out of the saddle, hitched the burrow to the rail, then collected his sacks and stumped inside.

Going down from his room, Vance hitched the guns in his belt a little higher. The last thing he wanted now was trouble. He had to get some information from this old-timer, but he knew that Carla Morgan would never forgive him for what he had said back there in his room and there was the nagging little thought in his mind that somewhere out there, Matt Devlin was riding the range, nursing a terrible grievance and probably planning his revenge. But with an effort, he put the thoughts out of his mind, pushed open the doors of the saloon, and stepped through.

The bartender glanced up quickly as he entered, then bent over the bar. The place was empty except for the old man seated at one of the tables in the corner.

Vance walked over to the bar without giving the prospector a second glance. The bartender pushed a bottle and glass over to him. Pouring himself a drink, Vance drank it down, then said in a low voice: 'That Marty Benson?' He jerked his thumb towards the man sitting alone.

'Yeah, that's him. A saddle-tramp. He always reckons he'll get a strike up there in the hills, but whenever he comes into town, the story is always the same. The next time, maybe. This time, he's had rotten luck. The seam he thought was there proved to be a mirage.' The other shook his head sadly. 'I reckon for Marty that the seam will always be tomorrow.'

'How does he live then?'

'Morgan seems to have a soft spot for the old fool. He always gets a bed in the livery stables whenever he hits town and a meal here. I don't know why he does it. I wouldn't be surprised if he hasn't got some reason of his own.'

Vance took a second drink and carried the glass over to the table, seating himself in the chair opposite the old prospector. 'Hiya, pardner,' he said genially. 'They tell me you might be the man to help me.'

The other glanced up at him suspiciously, eyes narrowed. Then he scratched his head solemnly. 'Don't reckon I knows you, mister,' he said hoarsely. 'Just what do yuh want to know?'

Vance lowered his voice. 'They tell me that you were the man who found that horse with the blood-stained saddle, the one that the Ranger rode when he went out into the desert after Hagberg.'

The eyes which regarded him grew cunning. He took a deep sighing breath. 'You want to git mixed up with Hagberg and his men?' He ran his tongue over dry lips. 'Pretty dry riding the trail today,' he remarked obliquely.

Vance turned and nodded to the bartender. The man brought the bottle over and left it on the table. Waiting until he had gone back behind the bar, Vance poured the

old prospector a drink, then went on harshly. 'What do
you know about that Ranger's death?'

'Now listen, mister. You ain't going to pin that on me.'
The eyes were mere slits now. 'Jest who are you – the law?'

'No, just interested. I'm working for Morgan, if you
want to know. My job is to run this killer down and that's
what I intend to do.'

'Then that's your funeral, mister.' The old prospector
drained his glass and wiped the back of his hand across his
lips.

'You're sure you don't know where that horse was
headed from when you found him?'

The other shook his head emphatically. 'Nope. Reckon
he must've come down out of the hills somewhere,
though.'

Vance raised his eyes. 'Why do you say that?'

'Red dust on his flanks and under the saddle flaps. You
only git that stuff up there in the hills.' He threw back
another glass of rye, then filled it once more from the
bottle, shoulders suddenly hunched forward, eyes narrowing suspiciously. 'I reckon you're still asking a lot of questions, mister. Was he a friend of yours? I did hear about
him being a Ranger and that he was out to run down the
Hagberg gang.'

'You know damn well he was a Ranger,' said Vance, his
voice deliberately sharp and vicious. 'That's why he was
killed.' He dropped his voice to a harsh whisper. 'But the
Rangers aren't the only ones who want that outlaw gang
broken up, and Hagberg killed. As I said, Morgan has
hired me to do the job. But I'd be crazy if I rode out there
without knowing what to expect.'

'I'll say you'd be crazy,' Marty Benson said. 'You ever
met Hagberg face to face? No, I reckon you ain't or you
wouldn't be taking on a job like this for Morgan, you'd be
heading right back out of town. From what I've heard he
has twelve notches on his gun and that ain't no exaggera-
tion. They say he's the fastest gun thrower this side of the

border. And the gunhawks who ride with him are all professional killers. Some joined him straight from the Confederate Army. The others just linked up with him whenever they drifted into this territory.'

'Could be,' muttered Vance shortly. 'I'm still mighty anxious to meet him, but at a time and place of my own choosing. I don't aim to be shot in the back or from ambush like those Rangers.' He eyed the other shrewdly. 'You spend most of your time prospecting in those hills out there. You wouldn't know where that gang is hiding out, would you?'

The other paled a little and sat straighter in his chair. 'Now listen, mister,' he said swiftly, gulping down the glass of liquor. 'Don't get me wrong. I've always steered clear of trouble. I know nothing about the location of that gang's hideout, believe me. If it's out there in the hills anyplace, then I ain't ever come across it.'

'I think you're lying,' Vance said softly. His eyes never left the other's face, watching every play of emotion. He knew instinctively that he was right. The other knew something that he either didn't want to tell, or was too scared to. Even if he didn't know the exact location of the Hagberg gang's hideout in the hills, he sure knew approximately where it was.

Benson shrugged. He moistened his lips with the tip of his tongue. 'You don't have to believe me,' he said gruffly. 'You go out there and get your fool head shot off if you want to, but not me.'

'Forget it then.' Vance nodded easily towards the half-empty bottle. 'What d'you know about Matt Devlin?'

'Morgan's foreman? Not much. He's a dangerous cuss. Better steer clear of him if you want to stay healthy around these parts. He does all of Morgan's dirty work besides hiring hands for the ranch.'

'Morgan owns a ranch?' Ordinarily it might have struck the old prospector as strange that a man hired by Morgan to kill Hagberg should know so little about him, but by now the old-timer's eyes were glazed a little and his speech was slurred. If he did think it was curious, he gave no sign.

'Biggest spread in the whole territory, about four miles to the east of town. Twenty-thousand head, I reckon.'

'And what happened to Clint McCord? I did hear that he was supposed to be running things in this town.'

'He was, until Morgan decided to move in. There was a gunfight here in the Golden Nugget saloon between Devlin and McCord. Some of the witnesses reckon it was a rigged fight. That Devlin shot him before giving him a chance to go for his guns. But I reckon there ain't nobody here who's going to go against Devlin and Morgan.'

Vance sat back in his chair. On the face of it, there seemed to be two men here, both striving for absolute supremacy over the territory around Big Wheel, but possibly for different reasons. Morgan owned all, or most, of the land, had the biggest ranch and herd and had now taken over control of the town itself, no doubt using Devlin to remove all opposition. Then there was Clem Hagberg, hiding out somewhere in the Badlands to the south, a bitter man, possibly nursing some kind of revenge against Morgan who was a Northerner, determined to take over the area for himself.

So far, he himself was concerned only with Hagberg. Morgan was perhaps as much of a killer, although in an indirect way but so far he had not been declared so by the law. No doubt they would get around to that sometime, but in the meantime his job concerned only Hagberg. It would be far better to string along with Morgan until he knew a lot more of what was going on around here. Besides, if he was in the pay of the powerful and unscrupulous cattle boss, he would be able to demand answers to his questions from a lot of people, knowing that they would talk more freely if they knew what was good for them, and would be more inclined to tell the truth.

For a moment, he looked at the other, now slumped in his chair, head leaning forward. All of that rye after being in the scorching sun with only the brackish water of the desert to drink, made its effect more pronounced than usual. Scraping back his chair, he rose to his feet, caught the bartender's eye and tossed a handful of money on to the bar. 'See that he gets a meal and someplace to sleep,' he said quietly.

'Sure thing, Mister Vance.' The other scooped up the money and pushed it into his pocket, watching Vance carefully as he strode out into the dusty street, allowing the batwing doors to swing shut behind him. For a moment, he stood still on the boardwalk pondering his next move. Finally, deciding that there was nothing to be gained at the moment in Big Wheel, he walked quickly to the livery stable. Heat hung heavy in the still air, caught up by the dust and held there, unmoving, while the sun blazed down on everything, shocking back in waves off the street. Several men sat with their backs against the outer wall of one of the other saloons their feet hitched high on the wooden rail. They watched the tall man narrowly, assessing him, appraising him. He turned into the wide, open door of the stables. The sweet, cloying stench of swale hay hit him forcefully as he went inside. A grey-haired groom wearing a dust-streaked apron glanced up.

'Going riding at this time of day, Mister Vance?' he said genially. 'Gets mighty hot outside of town.'

'Reckon it does,' agreed Vance quietly. 'But I feel like riding. Got to see a few things out there to the south.'

'You ain't going into the Badlands, are you?' asked the other, staring at him in surprise. 'Better watch yourself out there. Or mebbe you ain't heard of the Hagberg gang.'

'Sure, I heard of 'em.' Vance nodded and took his horse from the stall. 'Seems everybody in the territory has heard about Hagberg.'

'They're killers. Come into Big Wheel sometimes. When that happens, most of the folk just light out of town. There may be looting, but that's better than being shot down in the street. But out there in the hills, you'd be a sitting target for them. That's what must've happened to those three men they killed a while back. Rangers they were, I reckon.'

'You know what happened to those men?' queried Vance sharply.

The other shook his head. 'Don't rightly know much about that. They rode out into the hills and never came back. At least, the last man's horse came back into town, but there was no sign of him. Reckon he must've run foul of the gang and been shot in the back. Bushwhacked probably somewhere along the trail.'

'Thanks for the warning, anyway,' acknowledged Vance. He climbed into the saddle and rode out through the town and along the dusty trail into the hills to the south; along the trail which Matt Devlin had taken an hour earlier after talking with Carla Morgan.

There was something between those two, he reflected, something which seemed to have a definite bearing on this case. He wondered if Morgan knew that his daughter was in cahoots with his foreman. Somehow, he didn't think so. These thoughts, radiating from his brain, served to spark a sense of urgency in his mind.

He rode quickly once he left Big Wheel, taking the stage trail towards Twin Creeks. Then, a couple of miles out of Big Wheel, he turned off the trail, letting his mount relax as they wound their way between tall, jagged rocks, finally climbing to a long ridge of bare stratum. Here, he reined the sorrel and paused, looking down into the wild, barren stretches of the Badlands. They had certainly been well named. There was precious little water here and conditions were bad; a scorching sun by day and an intense cold by night. A man could burn to death in the daytime or freeze to death when darkness came. Or he could starve or die of thirst. He curled his lips at the thought. There were a hundred ways in which a man could die here in this terrible wilderness – and one way was from a bullet fired by Hagberg or one of his killers.

It was small wonder that the Badlands was the haunt only of wild animals, gunhawks such as Clem Hagberg and lonely prospectors such as Marty Benson, searching for a rich gold vein which would probably never materialize.

Shading his eyes against the wicked glare of the sun, he searched the rocks and gullies for any sign of movement, any indication of life. He saw nothing. Further to the north, just visible, the stage trail was a grey scar in the stretching wilderness: but closer at hand, there were a thousand places where a killer might hide. Stretching away southwards, the rolling ridges became a jumbled country of pinnacles, buttes and boulders that crowded together, tumbling over each other as if in haste to reach the spiking peaks of the Diablo Range, ten or fifteen miles away.

Climbing back into the saddle, Vance kept a wary eye on the terrain around him, as well as searching the sandy earth between the rocks and ridges for signs of fresh saddle-horse hoof prints. In places, he found some but they were smaller than those of the average horse and he guessed that they had been made by Marty Benson and his burrow when they had come down out of the hills into town.

Here and there, as he rode south, the trail, narrow and virtually indistinguishable in places, petered out completely and he was forced to guide the sorrel over wide stretches of rock. A gust of hot wind came up the side of the hills as he reached the top and began the slow ride down the other side. In front of him lay a long, wide valley and, at the bottom of it, a long-dry river bed, cracked by the heat where the white clay had expanded under the scorching sun and crumbled into dust. It was as he turned a sharp bend between two rearing columns of rock that Vance first noticed the cabin. Narrowing his eyes, he halted his mount and slid softly from the saddle, pulling the long-barrelled Winchester from its leather scabbard. Gently, he eased himself forward, moving from rock to rock, his head well down. He wondered if this could be the outlaws' hideout, then decided against it. The cabin did not look as if it had been occupied for many years and had probably belonged to one of the lonely prospectors several years before, in the days before the Civil War, when there had been widespread rumours of gold in the hills. Several men had headed out here in those days, fired with the ambition and desire to make themselves rich overnight. So far as he knew, none of them had ever made it. More than half of them had left, disillusioned and broken men, and most of the others still lay out here somewhere, their bones dry and bleached in the sun.

For ten minutes, he lay crouched among the hot rocks, feeling the heat from them soaking uncomfortably into his body, eyes narrowed to mere slits, as he watched the cabin. Nothing moved that he could be sure of, although once he imagined that he saw something flicker at the back of the single window, as if a man, hiding behind it, had moved a little to one side.

Some lonely old saddle-tramp who had found this place and decided to shack up there for a while? It was possible, but Vance doubted it. Nobody in their right mind would stay here unless it was for a very definite reason, such as to get away from the law. A few shrivelled cottonwoods thrust stunted branches in front of the shack, sucking what little moisture they could from the parched soil. For a moment, his hand slid along the butt of the Winchester, then, reassured, he lowered it to his side and stepped out into the open. To get to the cabin, he would have to walk across that bald space which lay between it and the nearest line of rocks. And in the full glare of sunlight, he would make a perfect target for any gunman who happened to be standing at the back of that window. The very fact that there was no smoke gave him little comfort. In this terrible heat, it was doubtful if anyone would light a fire, even for cooking.

He stepped out on to the dried-up river bed, braced

himself to move across it, then paused in mid-stride. From somewhere in the distance, possibly at the back of the cabin where he couldn't see, he heard the clink of a horseshoe against stone. Swiftly, he froze, then began to back away into the shadows of the rocks, but not quite quickly enough. The rifle bullet kicked up the sand less than a foot from him as he threw himself back into the rocks with a swift reflex motion. He was lying flat on his belly, the Winchester ready to open fire within five seconds of that bullet hitting the dirt.

A rifle barked savagely and another roared almost in unison, confirming what he had begun to suspect. There were at least two men in that cabin firing at him. Evidently they had held their fire until he was out in the open to make sure of killing him. Something showed for an instant at the window and he snapped a shot at it, heard a sudden yell and guessed that his bullet had found its mark. Without pausing to fire again, he moved deeper into the rocks, circling around the cabin. The firing had ceased as if the others had guessed that he was no longer in his original position and were waiting for him to fire again and give away his position, In this direction, the rocks were nearer the side of the shack and he could see the three horses tethered to one of the cottonwoods. Three men, he reflected inwardly, with possibly one of them badly wounded. That evened the odds a little, but the dice were still loaded against him. There was no sound from inside the cabin and he moved his position slightly so as to be almost directly opposite the door to the rear. As he had figured, a moment later, it opened slowly, a man's head showed for a brief instant as the other gave a quick look around. Then the man came out warily into the open and moved swiftly along the back of the cabin, pressing himself into the wall. He held his gun in his right hand, obviously intent on slipping into the rocks to the rear, hoping that he would be unseen from the front of the shack. Vance smiled grimly. So that was the idea, to get one man to slip into the rocks and take him from the side while the other two kept up continuous fire to keep him pinned down.

Very carefully he sighted the rifle on the man as he made to jump into the rocks and squeezed the trigger. The outlaw seemed to halt in mid-air, threw up his arms and fell flat on to his face, the gun slipping from his nerveless fingers. In the same instant, a desperate burst of fire came from the window of the cabin and bullets whined off the rocks close to his head, ricocheting into the distance. He lay quite still, listening to the shrill whine of tortured metal. Judging from the fire, he guessed that both men were still able to handle a gun, even the man he had possibly wounded.

Ducking low, he changed his position again. He had only one chance now to finish this. So long as he remained out here among the rocks, those two men could pin him down and if he tried to make it back to his horse and make a run for it, he did not doubt that one of them at least would be able to hunt him down and overtake him in this terrain. Both men would know the surrounding countryside far better than he did.

After a couple of minutes, he came out of the rocks close to where the body of the dead outlaw lay in the sand. Unless they were watching the door, it would be possible for him to get right up to the shack without being seen. Anyway, he figured, it was a risk he would have to take. As he moved forward, he glanced down at the dead man's face. It was one he had never seen before; a swarthy, cruel face, thick-lipped. The face of a killer, he decided.

Slipping forward, cat-footed, he reached the door of the shack. He knew that the man who had slipped out had not locked it behind him and, in that event, it was unlikely that it would be fastened from the inside. Cautiously, he stood there with the rifle in his hands, then laid it gently by the side of the cabin and slid one of the six-guns from its holster. If those men made a fight of it, a rifle would be too unwieldy a weapon to use in the confined space of the cabin.

He pushed gently against the door and was not surprised when it gave easily under his hand. Then he shoved hard and stopped under the low lintel, eyes taking in everything inside the single room in one glance.

One of the men stood at the open window, his back to him. The other lay slumped against the wall close by, his gun still held firmly in his left hand. There was blood on his shirt where the bullet had clipped his right shoulder. Swiftly, the man at the window turned, pulling the Colt round in his fist.

'Hold it,' snapped Vance tightly. 'Make one move with that and I'll kill you!'

He recognized the other instantly. Matt Devlin stiffened then allowed the gun to drop from his fingers on to the floor. Out of the corner of his mouth, he said quietly to the wounded man by the window. 'Lower your gun, Walt. This is Neil Vance. The boss hired him to kill Hagberg. We wouldn't want to do anything to stop that, would we?'

The injured man reluctantly holstered his gun. His lips drew back into a tight snarl 'He shot me in the shoulder, Matt. I figure he ought to pay for that, whether or not Morgan hired him.'

Vance fixed his gaze on Devlin. There was little to fear from the other man at the moment, but the foreman was always dangerous and Vance knew that he only wanted half a chance to draw on him and he would shoot him down for the humiliation he had suffered in front of Carla Morgan in the hotel room.

'Seems you've joined up with the wrong bunch, Devlin,' he said softly, keeping his gun on the other.

'What do you mean by that?' demanded Devlin sharply. 'And what brought you out here anyway? We figured you were one of the Hagberg bunch when you came riding down through the rocks. We had you spotted half a mile away and you sure seemed to know your way around these hills.'

'Then you figured wrong,' snapped Vance. 'And you

don't have to lie to me. This ain't one of Morgan's men. It's one of Hagberg's bunch, like that hombre I killed out there at the back. I reckon Morgan would like to hear about this very much. His foreman in cahoots with the outlaws he's set on running out of the territory. Could be that he'd be looking for a new foreman then.'

'Don't push your luck, Vance,' hissed the other, eyes narrowing. 'We could quite easily say that we caught you here with that *hombre* outside. It would be our word against yours, and I reckon I know which Morgan would believe.' There was a faintly mocking smile on his lips now. 'And don't forget, Miss Carla will add her testimony to ours. When Morgan hears what we could say, it'll be the finish for you.'

'That's what you think.' Vance tried to force conviction into his voice. Somehow, he had to make the other think that he held more aces in his hand than he really did. Then he reached a swift decision. He advanced on Devlin and made a quick motion with the Colt. 'Turn around and face the wall,' he said thinly.

For a moment, he thought that the other intended to refuse, to go for the remaining gun in his belt, then he began to turn very slowly. 'You're sure going to die for this, Vance,' he hissed sibilantly. 'When Morgan finds out what you're doing, he'll make sure that you never get out of Big Wheel alive and you won't die easy.'

'We'll see about that when the time comes.' There wasn't much time left and as Devlin faced the wall, Vance raised the Colt and laid the heavy barrel along the back of Devlin's neck. The other suddenly lost all of the starch in his legs and folded to the floor, striking his head against the window ledge. Out of the corner of his eye, as the other went down, Vance saw the injured man nearby going for his gun. His hand flicked down with the speed of a striking rattler, but fast as he was, the gun was still only half-way out of the holster when Vance whirled and fired. The other's body jerked momentarily, then slumped limply against the wall. His eyes were still open, staring up at Vance with a glazing expression of utter surprise and disbelief in them. The Colt clattered to the floor and there was a spreading red stain on the front of his shirt. This time, it was just over the heart.

After making certain that Devlin was out cold, Vance went back into the rocks, caught the sorrel and swung easily into the saddle. He hit the high ground again as he turned back along the trail to the north, towards the town. As he rode he tried to figure out just how Devlin was tied in with Hagberg and his men, and where was Hagberg himself while those two men had been parleying with Morgan's foreman, the man he ought to have trusted above everyone else? He didn't doubt that once Devlin came round and headed back to Big Wheel, nursing his anger, he would have a talk with Morgan and present his side of the case before he could do so. Even if he got to Morgan first, it was possible that he would not be believed, in particular if Carla put in a word on Devlin's behalf, which seemed more than likely.

Brow furrowed in thought, he tried to make some sense out of what was happening. He had been in town less than forty-eight hours and already so much had occurred that he was now in the middle of a feud between the two most powerful and vicious men in the territory and yet, there was an underlying current there which he could sense but not recognize. More and more, he had the feeling that word of his coming and of his identity had filtered through into the Badlands, and that a plan was being built up against him, as had undoubtedly been built up against the three Rangers who had ridden this trail before him.

There seemed to be no one here that he could trust implicitly. He had divulged his identity to the Sheriff in Big Wheel, but the more he thought about it and the more he knew of what was going on, the more he considered himself a fool for doing so.

At a steady pace, he rode over the rough ground, the

sun hot and uncomfortable on his back and shoulders, shocking back at him in dizzying waves from the rocks and sand. Here and there, wide chasms plummeted downward into darkness, into deep shadows which were never relieved by the sun even at midday. Among the tall pinnacles of rock, he rode quickly, keeping his eyes on the narrow trail ahead of him.

Once he hit the main stage trail, he stopped the sorrel and let it blow. High in the air behind him, a flock of buzzards wheeled in slow, lazy circles in the sky, looking for death out there in the desert. Every gritty, dusty, heat-seared fibre in his body had set up a mocking scream deep within him and he wondered how men such as Marty Benson ever survived out there under such terrible conditions. Swiftly, he scanned the desert in the direction from which he had just ridden, narrowed eyes searching through the harsh glare of the sun which seemed to have seared all of the colour out of the surrounding countryside, leaving only glaring yellows and whites. At first, he could see nothing. Then, somewhere in the distance, there was a cloud of dust, heading towards him.

The sight sent a little thrill through him. He judged that the riders were not more than a couple of miles from him, if that, and were coming up fast. His own mount was tired and blown after that journey through the rocks and that punishing ride back and in front of him, even now, lay ugly country all the way back to Big Wheel.

His spurs sent the sorrel bounding forward, charging ahead, hoofs thudding on the hard-packed ground as it responded gallantly, seeming to have absorbed some of the urgency which was riding him. How many men were in that tightly-packed bunch coming up out of the Badlands, he did not know. In the harsh sunlight, and at that distance, it was impossible to estimate. But he knew instinctively who it was and why they were there. Some, if not all, of Hagberg's men. They must have found Devlin unconscious at the shack and brought him round, learned from him what had happened and now they were out to make sure that he did not reach Big Wheel or Morgan alive.

He had covered less than a mile of the trail back to town when a swift glance over his shoulder told him that the outlaw band had hit the trail and were coming up fast on his heels. There was no chance of reaching town before they caught up with him and he began to think fast. Up ahead, perhaps a quarter of a mile further on a thick belt of trees and brush skirted the trail on both sides. If he could get in there, he might stand a chance of throwing them off his trail, then hitting it out across country into the town. He swung the sorrel sharply into the thicket as he came up to it, plunging headlong into the trees. Whatever happened, he had to get out of the glaring sunlight which would show him up for miles. Branches ripped at him. He changed direction a little, pulling hard on the reins. The brush between the lines of trees grew thicker. More branches whipped around him as he spurred the mount onward and he took a beating on the head and shoulders as he bent his body down almost on to the saddle horn.

Once he was well inside the thicket, he halted the horse so that there was no sound of movement. In the distance, he could hear the thunder of hooves as his pursuers came up on him. Once, he heard someone shout an order harshly, then the sound of hoofbeats slowed, grew less and he knew what had happened. They had guessed what he had done and were standing quite still, unable to see him, or make out the exact point where he had swung sharply off the trail. Now they were keeping silent, hoping to pick him out by any movement as he crashed through the brush. A shot blasted somewhere and he jerked round instinctively, then grinned to himself in the green darkness. They had been shooting blind, he told himself. He wondered if Devlin was there with them, probably insisting that once they located him, they were to leave him to the foreman. The clinging silence lasted for a few moments, then another order was given in the harsh voice and he heard the sound of horses coming towards him through the trees. They were not making as much noise as he had anticipated and he figured that they had split into two groups, with one bunch of men searching the thicket on the other side of the trail. At the moment they would not know in which direction he had gone.

Gently, he eased the sorrel forward as he picked up the sound of harsh voices behind him coming steadily nearer. It hadn't taken them long to figure out his moves, he thought bitterly, and this was not the time to stand and make a fight for it. These men would take no chances as far as he was concerned. They would shoot him down in cold blood as they had those other three men even though they probably didn't know his true identity yet. He broke out into a clearing but almost instantly hit the lay of tangled undergrowth on the other side. His face and arms were cut and bleeding in several places now, but he scarcely felt the pain. Everything was now directed towards getting out of here in one piece and losing his pursuers in the process. A man bellowed loudly a little distance behind him and there was the sound of a shot among the trees. The faint swish of the bullet as it ploughed through the foliage near his head spurred him on and told him that he had been seen. The men were closer than he had figured.

He dug the spurs into the sorrel's flanks once more and it bounded between the trees, oblivious of the whipping branches which impeded its progress. Another shot blasted the trunk of a tree just over his head and he whirled in the saddle, aiming swiftly at the shadow behind him. His first shot missed but the second found its mark and the man pitched forward, hitting the ground and rolling over several times as his horse plunged on, riderless.

Sand and sweat had worked its way into the folds of

Vance's skin, filling them with an itching ache that was both irritating and painful. The sorrel plodded forward steadily now, head down as it pushed strongly through the interlacing branches. There was plenty of shade here and the spicy, pine smell of the trees was a pleasant change from the terrible heat of the desert. But the thicket and forest could not last for ever and he knew that, now the outlaws knew in which direction he was travelling, it would not take them long to overtake him. He had to travel as quickly as possible now so that when he finally burst out into the open, he would have a good lead over them. He remembered this stretch of forest from his ride out from Big Wheel and estimated that he was little over a mile from the edge of town. The odds were still against him, but it was a risk he would have to take now. If he stayed here much longer, it would only be a matter of time before they hunted him down like an animal and killed him in cold blood.

The thought of what had happened to the three Rangers who had preceded him on this mission brought with it a saving anger that burned through him like a flame. Ten minutes later, he reached the far edge of the thicket, came out into the open, into the harsh glare of sunlight. For a moment, he was temporarily blinded by it, then he spurred the sorrel forward, felt it respond gallantly, bearing him away from the shelter of the trees. He deliberately avoided the trail into Big Wheel. That was the way they would be expecting him to take and the outlaw gang might waste precious minutes before they picked up his trail once more. Besides, he guessed that by riding straight across the mesa, it might cut off a quarter of a mile from his journey.

As yet, he had no plan to put into action once he reached Morgan. But that was a bridge he would have to cross when he came to it, he decided. There was no sense in filling his mind now with all of these problems. The foremost thing now was to get clear of these men before they got within shooting distance of him and with a tiring horse that was going to be tricky. He rode directly into a sandy cut that ran at right angles to the distant trail, beside a gummy water hole which was almost completely dried up. The sun glow, burnishing the sky over his head, filling the dust which still hung in the still air, was sickening and the heat waves that refracted off the desert all around him, beat in endless waves against his face and eyes, forcing their way into his weary brain even though he had his eyes closed almost completely. A few more buzzards wheeled in their endless circles overhead like strips of black cloth against the pale blue mirror of the heavens.

He kept throwing swift glances over his shoulder, but as yet the others had not broken clear of the trees. Perhaps, he figured, they were expecting him to be waiting for them, lying low in the desert, ready to shoot the first man to show himself and they were taking no chances. When they did finally show up, a small group in the distance, almost lost against the sunlight, they seemed to have lost almost all of the ground they had made up on him earlier and he knew that his ruse in the thicket had paid off. Five minutes later, as he neared the outskirts of Big Wheel, he saw that they had turned their horses and were heading back into the mesa. Either they had no wish to tangle with the men in the town or for some reason known only to themselves, they had no desire to force a showdown at this time.

He slowed his horse as he rode into the main street of town. A few of the townsfolk eyed him curiously with flat stares as he rode up to the saloon and slid out of the saddle, hitching the sorrel to the post. Wearily, he strode inside and went up to the bar. Running his tongue over dry, cracked lips, he said to the stout man behind the bar. 'Beer, if you've got it cold.'

'Sure we've got it cold,' the bartender said. He brought out a bottle from somewhere beneath the bar and placed it carefully on the polished wood in front of Vance. 'You look as if you've been doing some hard riding since you left this morning. Been out there in the Badlands?'

Vance nodded. There seemed no point in lying to the other. There would soon be plenty of folk who would know exactly where he had been and what had happened. Most of all, he wondered what Morgan's reactions would be. He could always say that he had gone out into the hill country in the hope of catching up with the Hagberg gang. Even if the other considered him a fool for such recklessness, it was unlikely that he would guess at the real reason.

He took the second bottle which the bartender produced like a magician taking a rabbit from a hat and sat down at one of the tables. The place was almost empty, with just a handful of men drinking or playing poker at one of the other tables. Inside the saloon, it was hot and all of the windows at either end of the bar were open to the street. The end window, not far from where Vance sat, opened out on to the main street and in the distance he could hear the sound of voices raised as if in angry argument. He glanced in that direction, but could see nothing. The bartender began to polish the clean stretch of wood in front of him with his cloth and Vance got the impression that the other had heard the noise too, and had probably guessed at its meaning, but was trying desperately hard to look as if he had heard nothing.

The sound came closer. It was almost, Vance decided, as though the whole of the town was out in force; and the one thought that popped instantly into his mind was a memory of something very similar to this which he had encountered once in Dodge. When a lynching party had gone through the streets, seeking for the man they intended to hang.

Out of the corner of his eye, he saw the bartender suddenly lift his head, his gaze flashing past Vance to the batwing doors behind him. Vance raised his eyes to the flat length of mirror at the back of the bar, saw his own face reflected in it, and also made out the batwing doors opening swiftly and a short, portly figure standing there.

Slowly, the sheriff came into the bar, glanced about him for a moment as though seeking someone he knew perfectly well was there, then lifted his brows as he spotted Vance and walked purposefully towards him, his hands hovering dangerously near to the handles of the Colts in his belt.

'All right, Vance,' he said sharply. 'You're under arrest. Are you coming quietly, or do you intend to make trouble?' Even as he spoke, he took no chances, but pulled the Colts from their holsters and levelled them at the other. Vance looked at him narrowly.

'Just what charge are you making out against me, Sheriff?' he asked acidly.

The other's lips cut a thin line across the middle of his face.

'Murder,' he said quietly and Vance thought he detected a note of triumph in his gruff voice.

'Murder.' He shook his head. 'You've got the wrong man, Sheriff, and you know it.' He rose slowly to his feet. 'I'm working for Morgan, or didn't you know that?'

'Sure, I know it. But that makes no difference as far as the law is concerned. Besides, I guess you ought to know, it was Morgan who swore out the warrant. Says you killed a couple of men out there in the Badlands. There's a witness jest in case you're figuring on denying any of this.'

Vance nodded slowly. 'So that's it. Matt Devlin, I reckon. Sure, I shot two men, Sheriff. I shot them in self-defence. They were both members of that Hagberg gang working in cahoots with Devlin. Does Morgan know that?'

The other shrugged, still keeping the guns trained on him, ready for any surprise move. 'I wouldn't know anything about that, Vance. All I know is that I have to take you in; and if you know what's best for you, you'll hand over those guns of yours and come peaceful. That crowd out there are all steamed up. They've been figuring on hanging you in the square right this minute.'

That would be one way of getting rid of him, thought Vance quickly, and this time, it would be done quite legally. He measured the other carefully, through slitted eyes, then pulled the guns from their holsters and threw them down on to the table beside him. Even though he could probably outshoot it with a man like the sheriff, he couldn't hope to get away from that mob outside; a mob that had probably been incensed by Devlin and Carla Morgan. He still doubted whether Morgan himself knew anything about this. It was probably all Devlin's doing, swearing out a warrant against him to defend his own actions to Morgan.

It was all so diabolically clever the way the other had framed him. And he would get very little chance to speak on his own behalf at the trial, even if they intended that he should live long enough to get a trial.

'That's better.' The other motioned him forward. 'For a minute there, I figured you were going to be foolish and try to resist arrest. No sense in doing that unless you want to get yourself shot.'

'I don't aim to do that, Sheriff,' he remarked thinly, 'not until I know who's behind this little farce. And when I do find out who it is, then—'

'Could be that whoever it is, doesn't intend that you'll be around to do anything about it,' muttered the other ominously, prodding him towards the doors.

Outside, there was a crowd of townsfolk, crushing on to the boardwalk and overflowing into the street. Somebody yelled something harshly in the background as Vance came out with the sheriff behind him.

'All right, men, make way there,' demanded the Sheriff loudly. 'I'm taking this man to the jailhouse. If anybody tries to stop me, they'll run the risk of getting themselves shot. There's going to be no lynching here while I'm sheriff.'

Vance heard angry muttering among the crowd as he walked forward with the Sheriff's gun in his back. It was fifty yards down the street to the jailhouse, and as they neared it, he spotted Devlin on the far side of the street, watching him with cruel eyes. There was a faintly leering smile on the other's features as Vance was thrust up on to the boardwalk. He had the impression that he wasn't finished with the other yet, by any means.

Inside the sheriff's office, the other pulled a bunch of keys off the hook and indicated the direction of the passage at the far end of the room. 'Along there,' he said roughly. 'And don't try any tricks. After what you've done, I feel like shooting you myself.'

'Listen, Sheriff.' As the door of the cell closed behind him and the other turned the key in the lock, Vance whirled on him urgently. 'Get word through to Morgan about this. Tell him I've got to see him right away, that I have some important news for him. He'll come.'

'I won't tell you again, Vance,' snapped the other testily. 'But Morgan already knows that you're here. He swore out the warrant. If he wants to come and see you at any time, he'll do it when he's ready, not because you want him to.'

'You know damn well that Morgan had no part in swearing out that warrant,' said Vance angrily. 'It was Devlin who did that. He's in league with Hagberg. I surprised him with a couple of those outlaws in a shack out there in the hills. They opened fire on me from the cabin so I defended myself. If I had been the vicious killer they say I am, ask Devlin why he's still alive now, why I only knocked him cold instead of shooting him there and then.'

'What you did to Devlin or those two men is no immediate concern of mine,' said the other harshly, as he turned on his heel and began to walk back along the passage. 'All I know is that my orders are to hold you here for trial. That's what I intend to do. You'll be able to tell this story of yours to the circuit judge when he gets here.'

'And how long will that be?' Vance shouted after him.

'No real idea. Could be next week or, on the other

hand, it might be two, mebbe three, months. Hard to tell. He has a lot of territory to cover, you know.'

So that was the plan, thought Vance, seating himself on the low wooden bench which ran along one wall. Devlin didn't mean that he should get out of here alive. It was difficult to see what perverted sense of vengeance had made him go about things in this way, why he hadn't come gunning for him in the saloon. But possibly the answer was that this way, there would be no danger of him being outdrawn and shot. This way the townsfolk would do the dirty work for him.

3

Lynch Mob

The sheriff brought in some food an hour later and placed it on the floor of the cell. He watched Vance carefully, and one hand was never very far from the gun in his belt as he stood close to the door while the other ate, chewing on the food reflectively.

Vance glanced up from the tin. 'Did you get word through to Morgan?' he asked thinly.

'Sure,' replied the Sheriff easily. From the expression on his face, it was impossible to say whether or not he was lying. 'He said to tell you that he'd see you at the trial. Seems like Devlin has been doing a lot of talking to Morgan, especially about what happened in your room at the hotel this morning. You're quite a man with the ladies, aren't you, Marshal?'

Vance twisted his lips into a tight line. 'You'd better keep your mouth shut about that if you know what's good for you,' he snapped. 'There are plenty of important people back at Dodge waiting to get word from me over the telegraph. And when it don't come through, they won't stop to ask themselves any questions, this town will be swarming with lawmen before you know what's happening; and then you'll have a mighty lot of awkward questions to answer.'

The other paled for a moment, then relaxed against the door. 'You don't scare me none, Vance,' he said harshly. 'I'm the law in this town and if you make any trouble, you'll be turned over to that mob out there in the streets and they'll soon make sure that you don't trouble us no more.'

'A lynch mob, eh?' Vance grinned, deliberately goading the other. He guessed that the sheriff was a man desperately anxious to show off how big a man he was, and it was not a difficult thing to get a man like that to do some talking. Vance had met this type of man before and knew how to handle them. He placed the tray on the floor at his feet and picked up the mug of hot coffee lying beside it. Sitting on the edge of the bunk, he looked the other over carefully. 'They tell me that Carla Morgan is pretty fond of Devlin. Could be that Morgan's foreman is anxious to make sure there's no competition. If he can get Carla to marry him, maybe that ranch out there will belong to him some day.'

The other smiled thinly. 'You got it all wrong, Vance. It ain't that way at all. Evidently you don't know Miss Carla.' He seemed anxious to talk now. 'I've seen her grow up out here, except for a couple of years when she was back east at some school her father arranged for her. She's a vicious woman, inherits her fiery temper from her mother, I reckon. Any man who marries her will find that he's got himself a wildcat with the brand of the devil on her.'

'Then why is Devlin so thick with her?' Vance raised his brows. While the other was in the mood to talk, it was essential that he should find out everything that he could.

The sheriff shrugged heavily. 'Who knows what goes on in his twisted mind? But I don't reckon it will worry you much longer. Doubt whether I can hold these townsfolk for long —.'

'You mean that you don't want to,' snapped Vance tightly. 'These are Morgan's orders, aren't they? A lynching so that it will look all nice and legal. Nobody to blame when the truth gets out. That's the way of it, ain't it?'

The sheriff smiled nastily. 'You could put it that way, I reckon. Now if you was to try to break outa jail and make a run for it, you might—'

'Save your breath, Sheriff,' said Vance heavily. 'D'you think I can't see what's at the back of your scheming mind. Or mebbe this is another of Morgan's tricks. The minute I make my break, Devlin will be there at the end of the street to shoot me down. That way, it would be even more legal than if you let that lynch mob get me.'

'Suit yourself,' muttered the other shortly. He stepped out through the door taking the empty tin with him, slammed it shut and locked it from the outside, tucking the keys into his belt.

Leaning back on the bunk, Vance listened to the sound of the other's footsteps fading into the distance. There was the noise of another door closing at the end of the passage and then silence. Slowly, a plan was beginning to form in his mind. Outside. through the narrow, barred window, he could see that it was almost dark. The sun had gone down about half an hour earlier, he guessed, and the first stars were just beginning to show in the dark purple of the sky. Now that he knew Devlin would be waiting for him if he tried to make a break out of the jail, he was forewarned.

Listening carefully, until certain that the Sheriff was safely out of the way in the front office, or perhaps across the street in the saloon, he climbed up on to the bunk, reached up with his arms towards the narrow window set high in the wall. Even by stretching as much as possible, he would only just reach the bars with his fingertips. Slowly, he forced himself to relax. He did not doubt his ability to squeeze through that narrow opening, but first he would have to remove the bars. Fortunately, the Sheriff had taken only his guns away. He still had the sharp long-bladed knife and to help start the plan into action, he hunted around the cell until he found a loose piece of timber which he managed to prise from the bunk in the opposite wall.

Setting this on top of his own bunk, he clambered up on top of it. Now he could reach the window easily. As he had suspected, the bars were solid enough, but they were set only loosely into the framework of the window and he began to hack away at their bases with the tip of the knife, forcing it in as far as it would go and then levering it with as much weight as he dared. Several times the steel blade bent at an almost impossible angle, but it had been fashioned and tempered well and did not snap under the strain.

Bit by bit, he removed the stone from around the bases of the bars, working as quietly as possible, his arms aching intolerably with the strain of stretching himself to full length. But inch by inch, the stone was being flaked and hacked away and the bars were becoming loosened in their sockets. How long he worked like this, it was impossible to tell. The air inside the small cell was cold now that the sun had gone down. but he was sweating profusely as he worked, gradually easing the first of the bars out of place with a wrench that tore at his shoulder muscles. He laid it down carefully on the bunk and attacked the others. Once, he heard confused shouting and yelling in the street outside and for a moment it seemed to be heading in the direction of the jailhouse. But it faded after a few moments and he guessed that the sheriff or Devlin had dispersed the townsfolk. He smiled grimly to himself as he went back to work, feeling everything now in almost total darkness. His hands and arms seemed to be on fire and he had the impression that his fingers were bleeding where they had been torn on the rough metal and stone.

Three bars were out of their sockets and lying on the bunk when he heard the door at the far end of the passage open. A light showed briefly as he climbed silently down from his perch and stretched himself out on top of the bunk feigning sleep, hiding the bars with his body and praying that the Sheriff would not shine the light from the lantern on to the window high in the wall.

Through slitted lids, he saw the stocky figure just outside the cell, the lantern held high over his head as he peered in through the door. He held his breath as the light shone full upon him, then released it in a faint sigh as the other, apparently satisfied, turned and walked slowly back along the passage. No sooner had the door closed again, than he was back on top of the bunk, thrusting the slender blade of the knife into the stone, prising it loose. Tiny flakes fell on to his upturned face as he worked, some falling into his eyes, half blinding him. But he persisted doggedly, knowing that this would perhaps be his only chance.

The late moon crept up into view, a thin crescent which gave little light to see by. Sleep threatened to deaden his senses and his eyelids drooped. The thud of horses' hoofs in the street outside jerked him upright, bringing him back to his senses. Matt Devlin's voice, although low and distant, came to him clearly from the moonlit darkness outside. The foreman said to someone: 'Reckon he ain't going to make a break for it. But if he does, I'll be at the head of the street near the General Store. I want you to take up position at the other end. He'll make a break through the front door of the sheriff's office. The sheriff is a fool and I'm not sure how far we can trust him, but he knows better than to go against us. If he doesn't let Vance escape, I'll have his hide tomorrow.'

'What if he comes out shooting?' asked the other man, his voice one which Vance did not recognize.

'He won't. His guns are there inside the office, but all the bullets will have been taken out by now. The same goes for any weapons the sheriff has inside the office. By the time he finds that out, it'll be too late for him.'

The second man uttered a low, harsh laugh. A horse snickered softly and vaguely Vance made out the sound of hoofbeats receding along the street. He guessed that the town would be deserted now. The lynching mob would have gone back to their homes, thinking that he would be safely locked away inside the jail for the night and that they could carry out their threat in the morning. But he did not intend to be around there by morning and the knowledge that Devlin and his unknown companion expected him to make a break for it through the front office, made things a lot easier. It told him something else too. The Sheriff was in on this deal. It seemed that Devlin must have some strong hold over the other to force him to expose himself to danger like this, just for the sake of shooting Vance down in cold blood.

He paused for a moment, both to allow the two killers to get well away, and also to allow some of the strength to flow back into his arms and shoulders. His fingers felt numb through working so intently with the tough stone but now the final bar felt loose in his grasp and he worked away at it persistently until it slid out of its socket with a faint grinding sound. He held his breath for a moment, until he was sure that the noise had not been heard, then slipped the knife back into his belt, leapt for the window ledge, caught it by the tips of his fingers, and pulled himself up with a wrenching of shoulder muscles. Sweat stood out on his face as he levered his slim, wiry body through the narrow opening. For a moment, he had the idea that he wasn't going to make it, that he would become stuck in the opening. He felt the rough stone scrape his ribs as he thrust himself through with all of the strength he could muster. Once through, it was a long drop to the street and the impact of his heels hitting the solid ground rattled his teeth in his head and shocked through his body.

He stood for a long moment with his back to the stone wall at the rear of the jail, eyes darting in both directions. The narrow alley was dark and very quiet. Very carefully, he made his way forward, snaking between the rearing walls of the houses on either side of him, heading in the direction of the main street. He had to have a gun if he was to stand any chance at all of getting out of this town alive – and even if he did manage to get that gun, where could he go? Certainly not out into the desert, into the Badlands where the Hagberg gang would now be waiting for him, ready to drop him the minute he showed his face.

On the other hand. if he tried to stay in Big Wheel, there would be so many enemies after his hide, that there would be no one he could trust. He decided to ignore that point for the moment and concentrate on getting himself a shooting iron. Without one, he could be the target for every trigger-happy gunman in the town that night. He moved like a cat in spite of the taut stiffness in his limbs but several times, before he reached the end of the winding alley where it opened out on to the street, he was forced to pause for breath. These men who were lying in wait for him were a lot fresher than he was and he hoped that this would not tell on him when the time came for instant action. The fact that the two men had split up was in his favour. They would be watching both ends of the street, keeping their eyes on the entrance to the Sheriff's office, ready to shoot at anyone who came out so long as it wasn't the sheriff. He could visualize the other now, sitting in his chair, seeming asleep, ready to be jumped, knowing that as soon as Vance put one foot outside that door, he was a dead man; a man trying to defend himself against two professional killers without any bullets in his guns.

Gently, he edged his way into the street. At the point where the narrow alley opened out into it, everything was completely dark but his keen-eyed gaze soon made out the shape of the tall figure crouched in one of the doorways near the General Store about twenty yards away. Too far for a knife throw, he decided, and pondered his next move. Somehow, he had to get within striking distance of the outlaw before he made his play. To move too soon could mean the end.

The killer had picked his position with care for it commanded an excellent view along the entire length of the deserted street. He turned his head slowly, but could see nothing of Devlin. Better take this man first and attend to the foreman later. Moving like a shadow, making not the slightest whisper of sound, Vance edged his way along the front of the nearby building, thankful for the over-hanging balcony which threw deep shadow on to the boardwalk. In the middle of the street there was a pale gleam of moonlight that painted a silver-grey river of dust through the town. Silently, he slid the knife from his belt, held it ready in his right hand. The other man had not made a move, he crouched there like a figure carved from granite, the rifle held across his knees. Vance shivered slightly as he realized what would have happened if he had escaped through the office, knocking the sheriff cold as they had expected him to do, and then stepped out into the moonlight in the road. One shot from that rifle through his leg, the useless guns in his hands, and he would have stood no chance at all. Out of the corner of his eye, he noticed the square patch of yellow light that showed through the window of the sheriff's office. It would have made an excellent background against which he would have been silhouetted, his body forming a good target. It was the only light that showed in the whole length of the street. All of the other citizens of Big Wheel would be sleeping soundly, unaware of the little personal drama that was taking place in their midst.

As he slid nearer, he saw that the other was more wary now, turning his head quickly up and down the street, as if expecting something to happen. The tightness knotted inside Vance's stomach. His apprehension had been mounting for the past couple of hours, since it had become clear that he would have to kill this man and possibly Devlin before he got clear of the town and the trouble that lay in store for him.

Seconds later, he crept up behind the unsuspecting man and thrust the point of the blade hard against the back of his shoulders, so that it went through the cloth of his shirt and bit deeply into the skin. He felt the other stiffen abruptly and draw in his breath in a sharp hiss.

'Just keep quite still and don't make a sound unless you want to die,' he whispered thinly.

'Devlin said you were in the jailhouse,' muttered the other softly, not daring to raise his voice.

'Could be that he's mistaken.' murmured Vance tautly. 'Now just lower that rifle on to the boardwalk beside you – and no noise or I'll kill you right here. And don't risk a yell for Devlin. You'll be dead long before he gets to you, I promise you that.'

The other had heard the tight trace of purpose in Vance's voice and knew that he meant every word he said. He paused only for a brief moment, then carefully lowered the heavy Winchester to the wooden slats of the boardwalk, holding himself tensed. Vance knew that he could not trust the other for a single moment. The instant he relaxed his vigilance, the man would either try to go for the guns in his belt or attempt to throw himself forward, away from the knife point. He wasted no time. Reaching forward with his left hand, he plucked the other's Colts smoothly from their holsters and thrust them into his own. Now, he no longer felt so naked and defenceless.

The man did not wait long to make his try. He lunged forward suddenly, head thrust low on his chest in an attempt to avoid being hit by one of the guns, knowing that Vance would not want to make more noise than he could help. Swiftly, Vance hammered downward with the Colt he had snatched from his holster at the other's sudden movement, reversing it with a skill and swiftness born of long experience. The butt glanced off the killer's shoulder, jarring him from head to foot, but not stopping him. His own momentum carried him forward a little way, into the moonlit street, as he sagged on to his knees, all of the starch going from his legs.

Like a mountain cat, Vance leapt after him, swinging the gun again by the barrel before the other could utter a single cry. The man went down on to his knees, then rolled forward, his wide-brimmed hat falling from his head.

Even as Vance knelt beside him, there was the sharp bark of a rifle from further along the street and the bullet skipped through the dust less than a foot from his body. Savagely, he leapt back into the shadows. The spitting flame from the rifle came again. Devlin had spotted what had happened. Now he was intent on killing Vance, caring little if he woke the whole town.

Swiftly, the lawman cast about him, judging the best way to go to get to his horse. Devlin was located between him and the livery stables and that made things difficult. A third bullet smashed into the wall of the store at his back and he dropped on to his stomach on the boardwalk. A moment later, the door of the sheriff's office was kicked open and the portly figure of the Sheriff appeared, framed in the opening. He carried a rifle in his hands and stared hard along the street, then began firing swiftly as Devlin came running up and pulled him back into the shadows.

Cautiously, Vance eased himself back along the front of the store, taking care not to lift his head. It would not be long before those two men out there plucked up enough courage to come and follow him. Reaching the end of the boardwalk and the far side of the store, he slipped around the corner and began to run. Behind him, he heard a savage shout, knew that he had been spotted for that brief instant when he had shown himself against the moonlight. There was the clatter of footsteps on the wooden boards as the others came after him. The sound warned Vance that he had little time for reflection. There was no chance of him reaching his horse now. To head back in that direction would be courting disaster. Devlin was an accurate shot with the rifle and if there were more men coming out on to the street in response to the sound of shooting, that was where they would be. They would open up on him at Devlin's command, not pausing to think. It was something he dared not risk. He was certain that his enemies still lurked around him in the shadows as he fled along the boardwalk, then raced across the open stretch of street until he lay crouched behind a rain barrel on the other side, both sixers in his hands, waiting.

Three men ran around the far corner of the street, hesitated, looking about them, sensing a trap but still not sure. They would probably know by now, after searching the unconscious body of the killer, that he had his guns. It was the snicker of a horse, not the sound of a footfall, that brought Vance tautly into a position of frozen anticipation behind the barrel. It came from somewhere just out of sight, around the corner, he judged; and a moment later, he knew what was going to happen. None of those men he had just seen as they had ducked back into the shadows had been Devlin. One had been the sheriff, he felt sure of that, but Morgan's foreman was still somewhere out of sight, probably on horseback, intending to run him down. He steadied himself and waited, resting one of the guns on the top of the barrel. A dark shape moved up on the far side of the street, edged into view. He saw the moonlight glint on metal as the man's arm moved slowly, bringing up the gun. Whether or not the man could see him, Vance did not pause to find out. Switching the gun around, he squeezed the trigger and grinned in sudden satisfaction as the man screamed shrilly and pulled himself back again, out of sight. Another man cursed volubly close by and Vance turned his head again, eyes peering into the darkness beneath the overhanging balconies which kept the boardwalks in shadow. The gun kicked and roared again in his hand as two men dashed out into the open, dropped on to their faces and began shooting into the darkness, their bullets thumping into the wood close to his head as he pushed himself down behind the shelter of the barrel. He raised his arm, cutting loose at the fast stabs of orange gunfire which spat at him out of the darkness around the store on the corner He couldn't tell how many there were

– less than half a dozen surely – because the man he had wounded, now lying on the street, nearer than the others, began crawling in his direction, shooting as he came. A bullet hit the side of the barrel and whined off in danger-ous ricochet. Instantly, he threw a pair of bullets at the man lying prone on the ground, saw him jerk convulsively as they bit into his body.

Restlessly, he edged back from his hiding place, crawled towards the wall, then got to his feet and moved around the rear wall of the building. There were too many for him to take care of. Once they took it into their heads to rush him, probably led by Devlin on horseback, he would be finished. The sooner he got out of there, the better. It was a close squeak to ease himself around the corner of the building, but he did it. There was a pause in the firing now. For a moment, he wondered if they were getting ready to rush him and a moment later he had the answer. The sudden thunder of hoofs beat at his ears as Devlin, mounted now, came into view around the corner of the main street and rode swiftly towards where he stood, pressed flat against the wall of the building. He loosed off a couple of shots at the man on horseback, but it was impossible to tell if any of the bullets had struck home.

Lead whistled past his head, hammered briefly into the woodwork. Then the men who had been crouched on the far boardwalk came in at a swift run. The portly figure of the Sheriff was, as Vance had expected it to be, in the background. He obviously did not intend to run the risk of being shot by the Ranger. Relishing his own safety too much, he intended to let the ordinary townsfolk do the dirty work for him.

Devlin had wheeled his horse at the end of the street and was heading back, taking care to keep to one side, so that he would run no danger of being shot by his own men. By now, Vance had reloaded with the cartridges in his belt. He moved quickly back along the boardwalk, feel-ing his way, ready to fire on anyone who showed himself in the street. But the others were still cautious. They did not intend to shoot it out on even terms with the Ranger. They knew him only as a professional killer hired by Morgan to bring in Clem Hagberg dead or alive, and when a man had that kind of reputation, it was the height of foolishness to try things on even terms. They were waiting for Vance to show himself before they came out into the open themselves.

A bullet dug into the ground close to him and he jerked round, eyes narrowed as he realized with a sudden shock that it had come from the other direction, from behind him.

Even as the realization came, the sheriff's voice yelled 'That you over there, Dan?'

Yeah, Sheriff. I cain't see him yet, but I've got this end of the street covered. He won't be able to git out this way.'

By now, the shooting would have aroused most of the town, Vance figured, and the deputy sheriffs would have been alerted. This was probably not the first jailbreak they had had in the town and each of these men would know instinctively what to do in a case like this. He pressed his lips together into a tight line. This was certainly the tightest spot he had ever been in, in the whole of his career and at the moment, he could see no way out of it. No use in trying to convince these people of his true identity. The sheriff and Devlin would see to it that he was shot down before he had a chance to show his badge to anyone. And the irony of it all was that these were ordinary, responsible citizens who were intent on killing him.

He snapped a couple of shots in the direction of the man's voice behind him, not really wanting to hit him, just to make him keep his head low for a while. A bullet gouged the wall and ricocheted along the street with a shrill whine. He ducked his head instinctively, saw the rest of the men beginning to edge their way forward, closing in on him now, urged on by Devlin and the sheriff. He was so intent on watching them, trying to judge their position

and where the greatest danger would come from that he
failed to hear the door behind him creaking open until it
was too late to do anything about it. A hand grasped him
roughly by the arm and pulled him backward, off-balance.
Savagely, he fought to free himself, to turn and bring his
guns to bear.

The door was closed softly as he felt himself being pulled
inside the room and a voice hissed urgently in his ear: 'For
God's sake keep quiet, you fool, unless you want the whole
town to know where you are.'
    He relaxed suddenly and abruptly. There was no danger
here. The grip on his arm was released and he turned to
face the man who had saved him. He saw a tall, grey-haired
man with eyes which he guessed usually twinkled with
humour, but which were now bright with purpose.
    'I'm Doc Manton,' explained the other swiftly.
'Thought you might be in trouble and figured this was the
only way to git you out of it. But you're not safe yet. They'll
soon guess what's happened and come here for you. You'll
have to get out the back way. There are a couple of horses
there. I'll try to get you away to a safe place where they
won't think of looking for you.'
    A hundred half-formed thoughts and ideas were
whirling chaotically through Vance's brain, but he could
not turn them over in his mind at that particular moment.
For the time being, he was content to do as the other said,
knowing that, somehow, a miracle had happened to him,
that he had found a friend in this town, and that he would
have to hurry if he was going to get away before Devlin and
the others came hammering at the door after him.
    He followed the other swiftly through the darkened
house, occasionally stumbling over a piece of furniture,
knocking his shins against chairs and a table as they
moved through the house, out through the door at the
back, and emerged into a small courtyard which opened
off into another narrow street. As the other had said, there

were two mounts waiting for them. Silently, the Doc motioned him to climb up into the saddle of the nearer horse, while he swung up expertly into the other. He moved quickly and quietly for a man of his age, and Vance guessed that he had done this many times before. From the street in the distance came the sound of shots and once Vance picked out Devlin's booming voice yelling orders to the men, urging them to close in on the spot where he figured that Vance was still cornered like a rat.

Vance smiled grimly to himself as he let the horse move forward slowly, making little sound until they were some distance from the house. Then he dug his spurs into the beast's flanks as the Doctor did likewise and they urged their mounts through the pale moonlight, through the narrow street until it opened out on to the main trail at the very edge of town and they were shaking the dust of Big Wheel off their heels.

They rode swiftly for several miles, heading across country, moving always to the north. Doc Manton seemed to know his way around and for the time being, Vance was content to let him lead the way. They hit mesquite brush half an hour later and pushed on through rough and rugged country, vague details of which showed up in the moonlight. They hit a narrow trail a little while later that shone faintly in the moonlight and began to climb into the hills. How long they travelled it was impossible to estimate. The wind was cold and raw and bit through his shirt in numbing waves. The blood on his hands had dried and was crusted over his fingers, so that it was difficult to keep his grip on the reins. Then, up ahead of him, he spotted the small shack, tucked away in a fold in the hills so that it was invisible from down below and there was only this single trail leading up to it. It looks an excellent place for defence, he judged. A man could hold out against an army here and he wondered how Doc Manton knew about it; and how he knew it would be unoccupied right now.

The other reined his mount in front of the shack, slid

easily from the saddle and waited until Vance had done likewise. Then he pointed and said quietly: 'I've found that this place makes a nice little hideout at times such as this. There are very few people who know of its existence, and those who do are not in league with either Hagberg or Morgan, so you can set your mind at rest on that particular point.'

Vance walked stiffly to the shack, paused while the other threw open the door, then stepped inside. There was a little furniture there, a pile of logs set against the wide, open hearth and a stove with a frying pan sitting on top of it.

'Make yourself comfortable,' said the other, motioning to one of the chairs. 'I'll fix us a bite to eat and some coffee. You look as though you could use some. Then we'll talk. I reckon there's a lot of questions you're just burning to ask. But first we eat.'

Vance nodded. He lowered himself into the chair and forced the muscles of his body to relax. His head cleared slowly and some of the strength came back into his limbs. Pretty soon, there was the smell of bacon frying in the pan inside the room and hot coffee bubbling away on the top of the stove. He leaned forward in his chair as the other pulled out a couple of tin plates and began scooping the slices of bacon on to them with the blade of his knife. He set one of the plates down in front of Vance and said quietly: 'Go on, eat it all. It'll put some life back into you. I can guess a little of what they did to you back there although I'm not sure yet why they did it. I suspect that Devlin and Morgan are behind it.'

He eyed Vance shrewdly as the other began to eat. For the first time, Vance realized how ravenously hungry he was. As he ate, the other went on: 'I heard about the way you beat up Matt Devlin in the hotel, and in front of Carla Morgan too. He must want to kill you pretty badly because of that. No one has ever done that to him before and he ain't the kind of man who takes well to humiliation, particularly in front of a woman. Also heard about those two men you killed out in the Badlands. It was Devlin who swore that you shot them in the back and attacked him when he tried to stop you.'

'And Morgan believed him, of course,' said Vance bitterly. 'I might have guessed that. I suppose Carla put in a word against me too, to her father.'

The other shrugged and sipped the hot coffee slowly. 'Could be, Vance. I don't know too much of what goes on at the Morgan spread. It ain't healthy to go snooping around there.'

'Why? You reckon that Morgan has got something to hide?' Vance glanced up and eyed the other intently from beneath lowered lids. The scalding hot coffee burned the back of his throat as he drank it, but shocked some of the warmth back into his weary body. He hitched the guns at his waist a little higher.

The other noticed the movement and smiled grimly. 'You're in no fit condition to go out there and challenge them tonight,' he said, smiling. 'Besides, I think you'd better rest up here for a while, at least until the heat is off in town. Once they discover that you've slipped through their fingers, Morgan won't rest until he's run you down.'

'Any reason why Morgan should do this. After all, he hired me to kill Hagberg for him. Doesn't seem the logical thing for him to do.'

Doc Manton pursed his lips, pulled out a black cheroot, bit off the end and spat it into the stove, then lit the cheroot and leaned back, blowing smoke into the air. 'I know what you're thinking,' he said quietly. 'That possibly Morgan is in cahoots with Hagberg. Somehow, I reckon you'll find that difficult to prove. They come from opposite sides of the border and there's nothing Hagberg hates more than a Northerner. Besides, they both want control of this territory and I can't see them agreeing to divide it between them.'

'So how do you figure it?'

'I'm not sure. But I've been in Big Wheel long enough to know that there's something between Carla Morgan and that foreman. Carla's the kind of woman who knows what she wants and will do anything to get it. She's hard and completely ruthless. I think she would even go against her own father to gain her own ends.'

Vance nodded soberly. 'I think I'm beginning to get the picture,' he murmured quietly. From what he had seen of Devlin, he guessed that he, too, was an ambitious man who would not be content with his present status if it were possible to get anything better. 'You figure that Carla has talked Devlin around to help her against her father and that they may be in league with Hagberg?'

'That's how it looks to me,' admitted the other. He put another pot of coffee on to the stove. 'I can smell trouble coming and I reckon that we've got a fight on our hands.'

'But just where do you fit into all this?' Vance tried to keep the curiosity out of his voice.

The other sat down heavily in his chair and ran his hand through the greying hair at the temples. 'There are a lot of decent citizens in Big Wheel who are tired of this constant murdering and feuding, who've lived long enough with the shadow of the Hagberg gang hanging over them and who want to see law and order restored to this territory. That's one of the reasons I helped you back there. The townsfolk were told by Devlin and Carla Morgan that you were one of Hagberg's men wanted for killing two of Morgan's trail hands back in the hills. It didn't take them long to stir the folk up to such a pitch that they decided to lynch you.'

'But Devlin was so mad that he decided to do the killing himself, but he wanted to make it look legal.'

'That's the way it looks to me.' The other was still serious. 'I reckoned it was kinda strange that those two should be so fixed on getting you killed, especially after Marty Benson had told me earlier in the afternoon that you had been hired by Morgan to put an end to Hagberg and his gang. Then I started figuring things out for myself. A stranger appears in Big Wheel and not long after three Rangers have been killed by the outlaws. Things seemed to tie in and pretty soon I felt that you were a Ranger too. That's the way of things, ain't it?'

Vance drew in a deep breath, conscious of the other's intent watchfulness, then nodded. 'That's it,' he conceded. 'I guess I made a mistake in giving my identity to the Sheriff when I first arrived. I figured he might be a straightshooter in this deal. Seems I was wrong on that count.'

'He works hand in glove with Morgan. He'd give that information to him within minutes of you telling him. Reckon he must have told it when either Carla or Devlin were there and they passed it on to Hagberg.'

Vance jerked up his head. That was a possibility he hadn't quite envisaged. It was bad enough if Morgan knew who he was and why he was there; but if Hagberg knew also, that made his position in Big Wheel and the surrounding territory a hundred times more precarious.

'I don't like this,' he admitted. 'It means there are two people I have to watch now, both of them gunning for me. So far, I've had no orders about Morgan. No doubt there are murder charges hanging over him too.'

The other smiled thinly, took the coffee pot from the stove and poured out another two mugs of the steaming liquid, pushing one towards Vance. 'I think you might find it a mite hard to prove anything like that directly against Morgan. He's too clever for that. Devlin has done all the dirty work as far as he is concerned. All he has done is give the orders.'

Vance stood up for a moment, took a turn about the small room, then came back. He spun the chair and straddled it, crossing his arms over the back. With memory of what had happened recently in Big Wheel, he had no doubt that the other was right in his supposition. First of all, he had to deal with Hagberg, carry out his original orders, then, if necessary, take care of Morgan. But he needed help and that wasn't going to be too easy in Big Wheel. He could no longer rely on his original plan of turning Morgan against Hagberg and bringing the other's ranch hands in on his side to help clean up the outlaws. Much as Morgan hated Hagberg, he did not doubt that Carla would be able to talk her father into killing him first.

'I know what you're thinking,' said the other suddenly, glancing up and studying Vance's face intently. 'You're wondering how one man can go out into the Badlands and finish off a vicious gang of killers. Am I right?'

Vance nodded moodily. 'I had it figured out when I first learned about Morgan's feud with Hagberg. Seems that won't work out now.'

'You'll get no help from the Sheriff either. He can't make a move without permission from Morgan.' Doc Manton got to his feet and fingered the gun in his belt. 'But I reckon I can get twenty or thirty men who might head out into the desert with you once I tell them who you really are. They ain't exactly vigilantes, but I reckon that's as good a title as any.'

'You're sure they'll go into the Badlands after that outlaw gang?' asked Vance in surprise. 'Seems they're getting kinda brave, all of a sudden. If they're as willing as that, why did they run away like scared prairie rabbits when the gang hit town a couple of nights ago?'

'I reckon you might say they've taken all they're going to take from both Hagberg and Morgan. You can push people so far, and no further. They've reached the point of no return.'

'Well, if you're certain about that, I'll be more than glad of their help. If you can get thirty men who can handle rifles or Colts, I guess we might be able to take care of those outlaws, if we have a bit of luck on our side.' Vance thought things over in his mind in the light of this new, and unexpected, turn of events. With thirty men behind him, he felt more confident of the future. At least they could deal with most of the Hagberg gang, even if they had to attack on the gang's own stamping ground – out there in the Badlands.

'When can you get those men together?' he asked, glancing up. There was a feeling of urgency in him now. 'We can drive out Morgan and his crew of killers if we try, but first we have to take care of Hagberg.'

'It ain't going to be easy. I'll have to talk to them separately. No sense in calling a meeting in Big Wheel. Soon as Devlin or Morgan hears about it, they'll come riding in with some of their hands and we may have a fight on our hands before we're ready for it. Can you give me until tomorrow night?'

Vance said: 'That'll be time enough. We'll ride out into the Badlands under cover of darkness. That way, we'll stand a better chance of taking them by surprise and I reckon we'll take Marty Benson with us.'

'You figure he knows where they have their hide-out?'

'Certain of it. He spends most of his time out there in those hills. I picked up his trail there the other day and it led right back into them. But he's scared to talk. He must've seen them plenty of times. If we take him with us, he may be more inclined to talk, especially if he sees that we mean business.'

'I'll see that he's with us,' promised the other. He got to his feet, hitched the gunbelt higher about his waist. 'I'd better head back for town now, in case I'm missed. You can stay here for the rest of the night and tomorrow, if you like. Nobody will ever think of looking here and you look as though you could do with some rest.'

Vance shook his head. 'I've got one other visit to make,' he said quietly, but with an odd intensity in his tone. 'But I'll make it back into town by tomorrow night and join up with you.'

For a moment, Doc Manton regarded him with mild surprise. 'You'd be a fool to leave this place. Here, you'll be safe. They'll never think of looking for you out here and you can lie low for a day.'

Vance nodded grimly, his mouth tightening into a hard line. 'They won't think of looking for me where I intend to go,' he said softly.

'You ain't figuring on going back into the hills, are you?' inquired the other tightly. He opened the door and peered out into the moonlit darkness. Everything was as silent as death along the mountain trail.

'Nope. I just aim to have a little pow-wow with Morgan. He ought to be at his ranch by now. Just to get matters straightened out between us.'

The other pondered that for a moment, then nodded. 'Good luck,' he said quietly. 'I'll get those men together and we'll be ready to ride by nine tomorrow night. If you don't turn up, I'm damned if I won't take them out into the Badlands myself.'

'I'll be there,' promised Vance. He waited until the other had mounted and ridden off down the trail, a tall, erect figure, dimly visible in the yellow moonglow. Then he went over to the other horse standing patiently in front of the shack and swung himself up into the saddle, ignoring the aches and bruises in his body. There was a lot to be done within the next twenty-four hours, he told himself fiercely, and the sooner he made it to Morgan's ranch, the better. But he would have to be careful and watch every inch of the way. Once Devlin discovered that he had succeeded in getting out of Big Wheel alive, he would lose no time in getting a band of men together and riding after him. He might also get word through to Hagberg, to let him know that their plan to kill him had failed and that they would have to think up something else to get rid of him.

He smiled grimly to himself as he sat still in the saddle, listening for any sound in the vicinity which might tell of pursuit. But there was nothing. Even the sound of Doc's horse had faded into the distance and a deep, enveloping silence lay over everything. Out here,

among the crags and rocky defiles, that silence held an
eerie quality and he shivered a little, not only from the
icy cold that swept along the ledges on the teeth of the
wind. He jigged the horse and kept a tight rein against
the bit, putting it slowly along the narrow, winding trail,
the urge strong in him to put the animal to the run, but
suppressing it with an effort, holding back to a slow
single-foot so as to make no more sound than was
absolutely necessary. He did not doubt that Morgan had
excellent men who could track down a man even in that
dim moonlight and men with sharp ears who could pick
out the sound of a running horse at a distance of several
miles.

He took a deep breath. If Morgan had men looking for
him, headed by Matt Devlin, it meant things might be a
little easier for him once he hit the Morgan spread. There
would be fewer men to take care of and he fancied he
might make it to the ranch itself without being spotted.
Whether he would find it as easy getting back out again
was something he didn't know. He checked the gun which
the Doctor had given him, made sure that it was fully
loaded, then thrust it back into the holster. He reached
the slope at the bottom of the hills half an hour later and
headed across the mesa in the direction of the Morgan
ranch. He rode like a ghost trying to slip away from the
moonlight.

Another half-hour and he was riding across meadow-
land, heading over a low ridge wooded with sassafras and
wild hickory. In front of him, in the long, stretching mead-
ows, the lush grass rose almost knee-high, thick and succu-
lent. It was good land this, evidently the best in the territory. Nothing less than that would be good enough for a
man like Morgan. Obviously it would raise the best of beef
and Morgan had plenty of head – several thousand according to reliable reports from Big Wheel.

As he rode, he had the grim premonition of savage
violence about to break out at any moment and he would

be right in the middle of it. There would be more complications, no doubt, and it looked bad enough already. He didn't want to overplay his hand, not right now, but that might happen if he was forced to show it before he was ready to make his play.

The moon was still high over the line of trees on the western horizon as he crossed through the boundary fence of the Morgan spread and headed towards the ranch, eyes flicking from side to side, watchful for any drovers there might be around, herding the cattle he saw on the ridges.

4

Savage Rebel

Pausing often to keen the night, the darkness and the shadows that lay on all sides of him, he was on top of the ranch-house almost before he realized it. It stood in a narrow, sweeping valley at the bottom of a gentle slope, the white walls glistening a little in the moonlight. He climbed stiffly from the saddle and tethered the mount to the lower branch of one of the trees. His limbs and muscles ached with the strain of the long rides of that night but a kind of urgent excitement seemed to have taken hold of him, something fierce and consuming that drove him on, making it possible to ignore completely the aches and pain in his body.

There was a long, low-roofed building a couple of hundred yards from the ranch itself. Even from that distance it looked deserted, but he made sure. Approaching it warily, his gun in his hand, he paused for a moment outside the solitary door, listening. There was no sound but none of the ranch hands would be doing much talking, he decided, if they were around. He waited for another moment, then kicked the door open and went inside, his eyes swiftly adjusting to the pitch darkness. It was the bunkhouse but there was no one there. Either the men were all out herding the cattle, or scouting the mesa looking for him.

He moved on, eyes alert. Over his head, the stars still stood out brilliant and numerous. Halfway towards the house, where a single light showed in one of the rear windows, he pondered on the wisdom of the move of leaving his horse so far behind. He might need it in a hurry if anything went wrong and having it at the top of the slope might prove both troublesome and dangerous. But equally, he doubted the wisdom of bringing it with him.

He was twenty yards from the rear of the ranch, almost directly opposite the open window through which the light shone, when he heard voices and froze in his tracks. Two shadows moved at the side of the ranch. turned the corner and came around into view. He recognized them instantly. Carla Morgan and Devlin. He crouched down low as they walked past within ten yards of his hiding place. They paused outside the house and he heard them talking together in low voices.

Carla said harshly: 'You're sure that he can't get away this time, Matt? If he gets out of the territory and spreads the word about Hagberg and the others, we're finished. He'll have half of the Rangers here within days and we can't fight that force, even with Hagberg and his men to back us up.'

Devlin's voice came clearly: 'You're worrying about nuthing.' He scowled, his face etched with shadow. 'I've got all of the men we could spare out tracking him down. Somebody must be helping him. We had him cornered back there in town, but he managed to slip through our fingers. The next time, I've given the men orders to shoot to kill. I'll pay them well for bringing him in dead or alive.'

'If it hadn't been for your foolish pride, wanting to kill him yourself, he could have been dead by now. The Sheriff had him locked away safely in one of the cells and it would have been the simplest thing in the world to get the townfolk so worked up that they would have lynched him. But no – you had to demand that it should be your bullet that killed him. So now, he's out there somewhere, free, knowing too much for our own good.'

Devlin rested his hands on the twin, high-hanging guns and glanced up into the darkness, seeming to stare right at Vance, where he crouched low in the underbrush. 'I wonder just how much he does know, and how much he really only guesses. We know that he's a Ranger, sent out to probe the deaths of those other three, but that's all. He's been talking to Benson. That drunken old fool may have told him something, but once he hits town, he thinks only of one thing and within an hour or so he's so drunk it must be impossible to get any sense outa him at all.'

'No?' Carla jerked her head up and stared at him. 'I still think he knows that we're working with Hagberg and once he's made that deduction, then he can easily guess most of the rest. Suppose he manages to get in touch with my father and asks him about all this. Where will we stand then?'

'I promise that they'll have tracked him down before dawn, no matter where he's hiding. If he's headed for the hills to the south, then Hagberg and his men will get him, there's nuthing so sure as that.'

'You've already sent word to Clem?'

'First thing I did as soon as I knew he'd slipped through our fingers. Hagberg ought to know by now what's happened.'

'He won't like it. If he comes riding into town again, he'll take the whole place apart to find Vance. And he may try to take out his revenge on my father. Much as I dislike him, I don't want him killed. That was the one promise I got from Hagberg when I agreed to go in with him. That he didn't kill my father. Run him out of the territory if he likes, but he isn't to harm him.' She glanced at Devlin narrowly. 'How many of the ranch hands can you really trust?'

'About half of them. I've been paying them double

wages for the past three months out of my own money. They know that there'll soon be a time when they'll have to earn it. I've been getting things set up for a time like this. I suppose we ought to have realized that we couldn't continue killing the Rangers one by one. Sooner or later, one of them would be a little too smart for us.'

'Better get those men ready to ride. There's no telling when we'll have to join up with Hagberg to fight Vance.'

Vance saw Devlin scowl and run a hand over his jaw. 'You figure that Vance will give us any trouble for some time?' There was a note of naked scorn in his voice. 'Even if he does get clear of the territory before my men catch up with him, it'll take him the best part of two weeks before he can get back here with any sizeable force. And by that time, we'll be ready for him.'

'You fool!' For the first time, Vance saw Carla Morgan as she really was. She swung on Devlin furiously, eyes blazing in the yellow light which came through the window. 'All of this has been your doing, and still you underestimate him. You admit yourself that somebody in Big Wheel helped him to escape. Whoever that was must know that he's a Ranger. And if. that kind of word can be spread among these vigilantes, or whatever they call themselves, then he has a sizeable force there already, waiting for him.'

'They won't fight,' scoffed Devlin. Some of his old bluster was coming back. 'And for God's sake, keep your voice down. Do you want him to hear?' He jerked his head towards the open window and Vance guessed that it was Morgan's room.

'Very well then,' she hissed savagely. 'Just remember who gives the orders around here. You keep those men ready and be sure that they can move out whenever I give the word. I want to be in a position to meet every eventuality. Pretty soon, we'll be putting in a night of real business and I intend to make sure that it turns out the way we want it. No Ranger is going to come poking his nose into our affairs and get away with it. We've ruled this territory for close on twenty years and it's going to stay that way. My father's getting too soft. Wants to run Hagberg out of the State and then set up some kind of law and order in the town. Figures he's getting too old to keep things going the way they have been so far.'

'You going in to see him now?' queried the other. His voice was calm now, the voice of a man unafraid.

The girl turned quickly. Her eyes gleamed in the light. 'Just to tell him that there's nothing to worry about. That there was a little shooting in town but it's all over now.'

'I'll get back to Big Wheel and check on any developments. They may have rounded him up. If not, that half-breed who's working with the Sheriff ought to have smoked him out of the hills by now if he's headed in that direction.'

Vance crouched low in the undergrowth as Devlin turned on his heel and walked over to the corral, saddled a horse in the dark and rode off. The single-footing died away slowly and he turned his attention back to Carla Morgan. She stood for a moment in the darkness deliberating, then pursed her lips and strode in through the rear door. Making certain that she was away, he edged closer to the building until he was crouched just below the half-open window. In the silence, it was easy to hear what the two people inside were saying.

'Was that Devlin you were talking to outside, Carla?'

'Yes, father. He's ridden back into town. There was a little trouble there earlier tonight. Some killer broke out of jail, tried to shoot the Sheriff and tried to escape. Devlin and some of the boys are out now trying to round him up.'

'You know who it was?' There was a note of tight insistence in the older man's voice.

Vance heard Carla laugh throatily. 'How should I know. Some killer, I heard.'

'I see. Seems strange that Matt should go out with the boys just to hunt down any killer. Surely the Sheriff could have got together a posse and taken that matter into his own hands, without Devlin getting into it.'

Whatever Carla intended to say in answer to that, it was never said, for at that moment, Vance raised himself swiftly and pushed his way over the ledge of the window, his right-hand gun out and levelled. He said: 'Could be that Devlin is so anxious, because I'm the man he's after, Morgan.'

'Vance!' There was surprise and a trace of startled bewilderment in the older man's voice as he turned sharply and stared at the Ranger. But most of Vance's attention was focused on the girl. She, he figured, was the more dangerous of the two at that moment. He saw that she was wearing a small pearl-handled revolver in a holster at her waist and that her hand hovered very close to it as he advanced into the room. His voice was hard and his eyes cold as he said sharply: 'Just keep your hand well clear of that gun, Miss Carla, unless you intend to ty to use it. I heard enough of your little talk outside with Devlin to learn several important things. You were quite right when you said that I'm a Ranger. I'm here investigating the deaths of those three men who were killed outside Big Wheel when they went into the Badlands after the Hagberg gang. But it seems that I've stumbled on quite another conspiracy that comes outside of the law.'

'I don't know what you mean,' snapped the girl angrily. Her eyes flashed at him and all the colour seemed to have drained from her face which was white and fixed with fury. 'All I know is that you're the killer who broke out of jail during the night and killed two of the citizens of Big Wheel, There's a reward out for you, dead or alive, posted by the sheriff.'

Vance smiled thinly. 'A reward posted by that sheriff isn't worth the paper that it's printed on,' he muttered tightly. 'And you know it.' He let his glance flicker towards her father. 'Seems I've been wrong about you in a few ways,' he went on quietly. 'I had you figured as working hand in hand with Hagberg and his men. Now I know that it's your daughter and Devlin, together with some of your own hands, who're in Devlin's pay.'

He saw the stunned surprise and then the slow look of anger on the other's face as the older man turned to face the girl. 'Why, you scheming little —' He choked off the words, then went on slowly: 'I always suspected there might be something between you and Devlin, but I never thought it was anything like this.'

'Don't listen to him,' said the girl quickly, her voice rising a little in pitch. 'Can't you see what he's trying to do. He isn't sure of anything at all, so he's trying to turn us against each other. That way, he figures he'll get all of the evidence he needs. There's no word of truth in what he says. Did he tell you that he was a Ranger when he took that job you offered him? No, he just said he was a hobo looking for work.'

'Quiet, Carla,' snapped her father quickly. ' I want to hear what Vance has to say before I decide anything. If he is a Ranger and I reckon he is, then one thing seems for sure – he's working against Hagberg.'

'And he's also working against you. Can't you see that? He knows about the way McCord died. It's common knowledge all over town that you ordered Devlin to draw on him and shoot him down in cold blood in the Golden Nugget saloon.'

'I told you to stay out of this.' Morgan whirled on his daughter, his thickly featured face livid with fury. 'Seems you and Devlin have been going behind my back for long enough. Now I'm just beginning to learn the truth. As for you, Vance, I've got no love in me for Rangers or the law. As far as Big Wheel and this territory is concerned, I'm the law and that's the way it's going to stay. If you want to stay healthy, then I figure you'd best use that gun and shoot me in cold blood here and now, because I'll come gunning for you if you don't. I've still got plenty of men here on the ranch who'll obey any order I give, in spite of what my daughter may think. I know there are a handful who're in Devlin's pay, but the others will do as I tell them.' He stood quite motionless behind the large oak table, his eyes never wavering as they met Vance's unflinchingly.

Vance knew that the other would be as good as his word, that even though he had known he was a Ranger from the moment he had ridden into town, he had only intended that he should carry out the work of killing Hagberg; and if he succeeded, that was as far as he would get. Morgan would have seen to it that he never left the territory alive to report back to Dodge. But even so, it had never been his nature to shoot a man down where he stood without having the other draw on him first.

He smiled thinly, tight-lipped. 'Thanks for the warning, Morgan,' he said drily. 'Now, at least, we both know where we stand. We're both caught in a very tight, cleft stick. You have two enemies, Hagberg in league with your own daughter, together with me; and I have the same. You and Hagberg. One of us ain't going to come out of this alive.'

'I guess you're right at that,' said the other ominously. 'I suppose that Devlin has already warned Hagberg of what has happened in Big Wheel?' It was more of a statement of fact than a question. 'I thought so. Just what do you intend to do now that you're here? Shoot us both? I think I ought to warn you that you can't get away from my ranch alive. There are plenty of men in the bunkhouse who'll come running the minute I give the word and they'll track you down before you've ridden a couple of miles.'

'A good try, Morgan,' said Vance softly. 'But I checked in the bunkhouse on my way here. It's empty. Seems they must all have ridden out on Devlin's orders. Could be that your authority around here isn't as good as you figured it was.'

Curiously, the other showed no surprise. There was not a single flicker of a muscle on his features at the news. Then Vance knew why. The other had scarcely been listening to what he had said. Instead, he had been straining to pick up some other sound outside; and now Vance heard it too. Distant and faint, but coming nearer, the sound of horses galloping quickly through the darkness. Morgan's men, heading back to the ranch. Possibly not the whole of the bunch, but enough to make it impossible for him to take care of them all, unaided. He saw the look in the girl's face and swung the other gun out of its holster to cover her. His voice was tight, like the lash of a whip in the silence of the room as he snapped: 'Take that gun out of its holster, Carla, by the fingertips and drop it on to the floor. Any wrong move and I'll be forced to shoot you.'

She must have seen the grimness in his face for she complied reluctantly dropping it on to the floor, her lips pressed into a tight, angry line. Even in anger, there was something coldly beautiful about this dark-haired girl. It seemed such a pity that she had gone wrong, he reflected. Whether it had been all her doing, or whether she had fallen under Devlin's influence, it was impossible for him to decide.

'Good. Now kick it over to me,' he ordered.

For a moment, he thought she was going to refuse. Then, with a savage movement, she kicked it across the carpet towards him. Holstering one of his guns, he bent to pick it up, pushing it into his belt. At that movement, in the split second when his gaze was averted, Morgan saw his chance of making his play. Even though Vance had been expecting the move, since the other was aware that help was very close, Morgan had the long-barrelled revolver out of the drawer of the desk and almost levelled on him before he swung up his own gun and fired. Carla Morgan uttered a shrill little cry as her father pitched forward across the oak desk, the gun slipping from his nerveless fingers and clattering to the floor.

Swiftly, he whirled on her as she started forward across the room. 'Stay where you are,' he snapped harshly. 'I only shot him in the shoulder. I don't want him dead at the moment. It isn't because I'm feeling big-hearted, but I may need him alive to testify at his own trial. That's the only reason I didn't shoot to kill.' He backed swiftly towards the window through which he had climbed. The sound of horses was very close now. He figured that the riders could not be more than half a mile away. It was time to get out of there – and fast.

'Don't try to follow me,' he warned thinly, 'or I'll be forced to kill you.'

He swung himself lithely over the narrow window-ledge, dropped lightly into the yard at the back and turned swiftly, running for the underbrush. He doubted whether Carla Morgan would be foolish enough to try to follow him herself. She would be relying on the fact that the riders heading for the ranch would have heard that shot and would come a-running.

Swiftly, he plunged through the cottonwoods, out into the open. From somewhere behind him, a gun barked and another roared viciously in the darkness. Ahead of him, as he stumbled forward as quickly as he could, the breath gasping in his lungs, the dawn was beginning to brighten and he realized that he would make an excellent target when he was forced to clamber up that draw to his horse. He ran half doubled to make himself small, twisting and weaving desperately from side to side. This was no time to turn and fight back. The riders undoubtedly outnumbered him by possibly twenty-to-one. He reached his horse in a sudden burst of desperate speed. Behind him, the pack were coming at a trot, but finding it difficult to urge their mounts forward through the scrub and over the rough ground. To his right, a half-dozen riders rode forward in a line to try to head him off.

A kick of his spurs sent the horse charging ahead, all the way along the narrow gully, then out into the open meadow. The way ahead of him lay clear, but in that emptiness lay most of his danger. The men behind him could see him for close on three miles, He would be forced to cover that distance before he reached any point where he could swerve off the trail without being seen by his pursuers.

As he rode, he cursed the fiery red glow that was beginning to flame along the eastern horizon directly in front of him where the sun was beginning to come up. Pretty soon, it would be light enough for the men riding hard on his heels to see every detail clearly for miles. He rode on swiftly for perhaps two hundred yards, then pulled hard on the bridle, turning the horse sharply to the left. As he swung, he increased his pace. More shots sounded behind him and there were several men shouting as they rode. Whether or not they realized what had happened, he did not know, but they must have seen enough, or guessed enough, to realize that whatever happened, he had to be stopped.

He swerved again further on, digging in spurs and punishing his mount cruelly Two more shots blasted and he risked a quick glance over his shoulder. The men were riding bunched tightly together, less than half a mile away, coming up quickly behind him. The smaller group which had swung wide of the main party to head him off had dropped back to join the other, after realizing that he had avoided that danger.

A bullet screeched over his back as he bent low in the saddle and he heard the savage blast of the report. They seemed to be gaining on him with every passing second and the wooded ground, which was his only hope, still lay the best part of a mile ahead, to his right. He swung the horse again to throw anyone behind him off his aim. Another shot was fired, but the bullet missed him.

'There he goes,' yelled a voice harshly. 'Stop him before he gets to the trees or we'll lose him.'

Vance gritted his teeth and eased one of the guns from its holster. He had to get out of this open, rolling country, if he was to stand any chance at all. Twisting expertly in the saddle, he threw two swift shots behind him. One of the leading riders suddenly threw up his arms and tumbled sideways out of the saddle. His riderless horse plunged onward, outstripping the others now that it no longer carried the burden of its rider.

But the rest of the ranch hands continued to come on, slowly but inexorably lessening the intervening distance. Vance threw a swift glance ahead. The wood was now quite close. Turning the horse very slightly, he headed straight for it. Another man bellowed something which was lost in the thunder of hoofs. Then he had plunged inside the trees, along a narrow, winding trail in the gloom which still lay under the thickly interlacing branches. He prayed that the horse would not stumble and lose its footing now or everything would be finished. Branches slapped at his face and shoulders, threatening to unseat him from the saddle. Behind him, he heard the crashing of his pursuers as they came into the trees after him. But they would not all come on his trail. They were too clever for that. Some of them would head around the wood, skirting the trees and move up quickly to the east, ready for him when he broke cover again. The thought spurred him on. There would be little chance of pulling the same Indian trick here as he had before when Hagberg's men were after him. These men knew every inch of this territory and they would hunt him down like a rat if he tried to hide among the trees.

Reaching a sudden decision, he cut off the trail, headed the horse deliberately into the thickest part of the undergrowth, moving to the south, cutting back in the direction he had just ridden, hoping to throw the other riders off the scent. This was the last direction they would figure him to take. The yelling of the men behind him momentarily gave way to silence as he pulled away from them. He guessed it was as he had suspected. They had been deliberately herding him in the direction they wanted him to go, knowing that the others would be ready to meet him when he came out into the open again.

For the moment, it seemed he had thrown them off his scent. The sound of hoofs died away now to the east and he moved more slowly, conserving the horse's strength and wind, knowing that he might need every ounce of speed he could get out of the animal very soon.

When he finally reached the edge of the wood, he found that it was almost broad daylight. The sun had cleared the eastern horizon, big and red and there was a fresh warmth in the air which relaxed his aching limbs. He sucked in deep breaths of the sweet-smelling air and looked about him with eyes that felt a little clearer than before. He was less than two hundred yards from the boundary fence of the spread and there was no sign of the others. They must have been so confident that they had him trapped that they had never considered this possibility and had left this side of the range unwatched.

Deliberately, he trampled down a stretch of fencing, then touched spurs to his mount and cut across country. Half a mile ahead, he reached a narrow stream and rode into it, urging the horse along it for several hundred yards before he clambered out on to the bank on the far side. It would throw his pursuers off the scent for a little while, anyway, he thought wearily. Perhaps long enough for him to reach that shack in the hills and wait for nightfall. Doc Manton had promised him that he would be safe there and he saw no reason why he should doubt the old man.

As he rode, he turned recent events over in his mind. He had discovered some of the things he needed to know during his short talk with Morgan, and he had also learned some things which were disturbing. Carla Morgan had shown far more shrewdness than he had given her credit for and the fact that she suspected the vigilante organization in Big Wheel for his escape was a little too close to the truth for his liking. If anything should go wrong with Doc Manton's attempt to get those twenty or thirty men together for that night, everything could be lost.

On the other hand, the fact that he had shown up at the ranch with no men backing him might have allayed her fears in that direction sufficiently for her to forget about that point for the present. He sincerely hoped so. Now everything depended on Doc Manton, on his ability to get those men together in utter secrecy. There were bound to be plenty of Devlin's men in Big Wheel, still searching for him and if they encountered anything suspicious, they would let Devlin know immediately. And the big foreman could put two and two together and come up with four as well as anyone else in the territory.

He controlled the rising feeling of tension and urgency inside him as he headed for the hill country. He seemed to have thrown his pursuers off the scent for the time being and he doubted if they would be able to follow his trail across this kind of country. Even the half-breed, that Devlin had spoken of, could not track a man across rock.

The sun was high in the sky by the time he reached the narrow trail leading up to the shack. From that height, he could look down on to the wide stretch of the valley below him, but although he saw a small cloud of dust far to the east in the direction of the Morgan spread, there was no one closer than that and he knew himself to be safe. He tethered the horse outside the shack, then went inside. Everything was exactly as he had left it. The pot of coffee was still on the stove which was now cold but within minutes, he had built it up again and had pulled some bacon out of the cupboard, frying several pieces for himself in the pan. When he had finished eating, he dropped down on to the bunk in the corner and allowed himself to relax. There was now nothing for him to do until nightfall when he would make his way down into Big Wheel and join up with the vigilantes.

After a few moments, he fell into a deep, dreamless sleep, waking refreshed with the sun long past its zenith, just beginning to dip towards the western horizon. He got to his feet, checked outside, then brought out some jerked meat and biscuit and ate quickly. Outside, the heat of the day was beginning to dissipate a little and already there was a cooler breeze blowing off the top of the hill, sighing down into the valley. He stood for several moments, staring out over the valley which stretched away in front of him to where it met the purple haze along the horizon. This could be a lovely place, he thought to himself, if only it weren't for men like Morgan and Hagberg. A place where men and women could come and build new lives for themselves. Perhaps someday, law and order would come to this wide and open country and bring peace to these rolling plains, lush valleys, and tall, sky-rearing mountains. The railroads might come through this place and no longer would it be a simple frontier town, but a huge city, teeming with people and wealth But until that day dawned, there would be a lot of trouble and death here, men fighting each other for control of the cattle prairie, for the right of way down to the river and then across to the border.

He sighed, threw a swiftly appraising glance at the sun where it was lowering in a mass of fiery red clouds towards the western horizon. For a moment, he had the feeling that this was surely an omen of what was to come in the next few hours. If they succeeded in locating the Hagberg gang and were fortunate enough to take them by surprise, there were still bound to be casualties on both sides. He felt a little guilty at asking the ordinary townsfolk of Big Wheel to go out and possibly be killed for him. After all, this was really his job. True, the people were protecting themselves for matters had to come to a head sometime, but he wondered how many of them knew what they were letting themselves in for.

These thoughts, radiating from his mind, drove him on as he went back and unhitched the horse. The animal had rested all day and was now completely fresh, ready to tackle the hard trail which lay ahead.

At a steady pace, he rode down over the rough ground, keeping his eyes alert for any sign of movement. Devlin would not have given up searching for him yet, and much as Carla Morgan hated her father, she too would be nursing revenge, and would spare no effort to track him down and kill him. And he fancied that she was more dangerous than Devlin. Far more shrewd and filled with an animal-like cunning which more than compensated for the fact that she was a woman.

He rode into the edge of the desert which lay at the bottom of the hills. There was no sound as he rode apart from an occasional whistle from some bird in the bushes and the rustle of a coyote as it slunk through the lengthening shadows on its nocturnal outing in the brush. Among the boulders which littered the lower trail he rode quickly, the mounting urgency inside his mind spurring him on. He did not push the horse, but allowed it to keep its own head. It was not until he had been riding for almost an hour that he came upon the remains of the fire which had been lit among the rocks. He smelled the faint trace of smoke on the air a few moments before he rode up to it, halting his mount as he stared down at the grey embers, his lips tightening into a grim line. The prairie trail started less than a quarter of a mile away and he guessed that the riders had stopped there to eat and not long before. Sliding out of the saddle, he felt the ashes with his fingers. They were still warm, as he had suspected. All of the Indian qualities of his training were uppermost in his mind as he scouted the area, every sense at its highest pitch. Once something slithered away in the near distance and he whirled sharply, gun whispering from its holster. But it was only a prairie rabbit that hopped away through the brush at his sudden movement.

Relaxing, he climbed back into the saddle, thrust the gun back into its holster and rode on, feeling a trifle uneasy in his mind. It was possible that these men had merely been cowhands out seeking strays for Morgan and they had halted here for their afternoon meal. But that seemed too much of a coincidence for his liking and it was impossible to rid his mind of the idea that these were the men who were out hunting for him and that, even now, they were somewhere in the neighbourhood.

He rode more slowly than he had intended now, eyes

and ears alert, keeping a tight, short grip on the reins, guiding his horse between the tall, rearing boulders. It was a terrible trail, made all the more difficult now because he had to make as little noise as possible as he moved among the long, black shadows thrown by the setting sun. He guessed that this trail was little used. In places, it almost dropped down to the point where it joined the buttes trail which ran south, directly into the stretching Badlands, clear to the Diablo Mountains.

Why anyone should have blazed a trail such as this was something he did not know – nor who had built that shack high in the mountains which only Doc Manton seemed to know about. Possibly it was some old prospector's cabin which had long since been forgotten; but even that did not seem to fit. It was more luxuriously fitted out than any prospector's cabin had any right to be.

He was still turning these thoughts over in his mind when he heard voices close by and instantly reined his horse, holding his hand tightly over the animal's mouth to prevent it from sending out any answering call to any other mount that might be in the vicinity. Sweat worked its way down his forehead and into his eyes as he remained motionless for what seemed an eternity, seeking with eyes and ears to pick out the whereabouts of those men he had just heard. Slipping out of the saddle, he dropped lightly to the hard ground and worked his way forward on foot, silent as an Indian brave. This time, he could allow nothing to stop him from getting through. Those men of the vigilantes would be waiting for him soon in Big Wheel, depending upon him to get through to them. If he didn't show up, there might never be another chance of fighting the Hagberg gang. He doubted if these men would have sufficient courage to go out on their own in spite of what Doc Manton had asserted.

Lifting his head over one of the tall boulders, he caught his first glimpse of the three men. They were clustered around a small fire, sitting on their haunches, their mounts tethered to a couple of stunted bushes fifty feet away, chewing at the almost non-existent grass which grew sparsely in this area.

In one swift, all-encompassing glance, he took in the fact that they clearly suspected nothing of his presence there and there did not seem to be any others nearby. Swiftly, he debated the chances of taking these three men and quickly. Tightening his lips, he realized that, whatever his thoughts might be on that point, it was something he would have to do. From a dense pine thicket, a whippoorwill started whistling over and over. Suddenly in the middle of its shrill note, it stopped and in the silence, Vance stepped out around the boulder, advanced towards the three men around the fire with both guns out.

'Hold it there,' he said sharply, commandingly.

One of the men, disregarding his order, went for his waist guns. Vance swung on him swiftly. 'Don't make that move unless you want to die,' he said tonelessly.

The man paused, then withdrew his hands reluctantly and held them where they could both be seen. Evidently, he didn't want to take the chance of trying to outshoot this tall, menacing figure who stood over them, his face grim and fixed with purpose. Slowly, not once removing his gaze from the three men, knowing that to do so for a single instant could mean his death, he moved around a juniper bush and stood over the fire, straddle-legged.

The tallest of the men, pale-blue eyes focused on his, had a half grin on his thin lips. 'This a hold-up, mister?' he asked tersely.

'You might call it that,' agreed Vance easily. He had the idea that sooner or later, one of these three would make another try for his gun; but there was little time to waste now. He had to hurry and that made him more of a fighting machine than before.

'You're a long way from your own territory, aren't you? Seems to me that you're Morgan's men and that was one of your fires I passed back there on the trail, a mile or so away. Looking for somebody?'

'Ain't no business of yours what we're doing,' snarled a thick-set man tersely. He licked the edge of his mouth with quick, hurried movements of his tongue. 'This country is free prairie as far as we're aware. We're out herding strays in for Morgan, sure.'

'Don't see any around.' He seemed to reflect on that for a moment. 'Couldn't be that Devlin sent you out to hunt down a man who escaped from jail last night, I guess.'

The angry expression in the tall man's eyes gave way swiftly to one of recognition. 'So you're Vance,' he said thinly. 'I suppose I should have known the minute you came in here with a gun in each hand. If you're figuring on getting away, reckon you'd better forget it. You won't get far, even if you shoot the three of us.'

'Get on your feet,' snapped Vance sharply. He made a menacing move with the gun in his right hand and the others jumped to it. Out of the corner of his eye, he noticed that the thick-set man was edging his way to one side, so as to get at the back of him. Vance knew what was coming next and was ready for it. Before the man was able to go for his gun, he whirled, swinging one arm as he came round. The barrel of the gun, held at arm's length, struck the other on the point of the chin and he went down as if pole-axed, stretched out his full length on the hard ground. As quickly as he had swung, Vance turned, backing off a little so that he could watch the two other men. The third man had not moved at all, but even as he turned he saw the other man make a right-handed drop for his Colt. The move worked in nicely with the plan which had formed in Vance's mind. Even before the other man's gun came out, he squeezed the trigger of his own, saw the other's arm jerk as the bullet hit his gun wrist, the gun flying high into the air.

Vance cast his eyes over them. 'If you want to do things

the hard way I'll be glad to oblige,' he murmured. 'Now turn round – and fast.'

This time, they both obeyed. There was no time to do things by halves, even if he had been in the mood to do so. These men were evidently paid killers, out to hunt him down. If the guns had been in the other hands, he would have been dead by now, lying there as carrion-meat in the rocks. He reversed his left-hand gun swiftly and struck twice, stepping back as both men sagged at the knees, then pitched forward into the dry earth. The third man was still unconscious, where he had fallen. Swiftly, Vance went over to the tethered horses, pulled the ropes from off the saddle packs, went back, and expertly tied all three safely so that there was little chance of them escaping, even when they recovered consciousness. They would probably be found sometime by their companions, after they had been missed for a little while.

He left them there at their own fireside and slipped back into the rocks, pulling himself into the saddle. For a moment, he threw a quick glance over the scene before riding off towards Big Wheel. Now, he rode swiftly, putting the horse into a full gallop. As he rode, he ignored the fact that he was probably leaving a clear trail behind him. Very soon, if everything panned out all right, Hagberg and his gang of outlaw gunslammers would have been cleaned up and he would be in a strong position for running Morgan and his men out of the territory.

It was almost dark by the time he came within sight of the town. He had passed no one else on the trail, even when he had crossed around the edge of Morgan's spread. Something was afoot and he felt more and more uneasy as he came nearer to Big Wheel.

There were few people on the streets as he rode into town, Stetson pulled low over his eyes to hide his face as much as possible. Even in the darkness, he did not want to run the risk of being recognized until he was good and ready. If any of Devlin's men were abroad in town, or the sheriff was on the lookout, it was essential to his plans that they should not spot him.

But most of the people around were ordinary townsfolk, a few women in their poke bonnets, evidently homesteaders who had ridden in from the east, and were passing through on their way to the rich lands of South California. There was nothing to fear from them. He saw three men standing in front of the sheriff's office. From the look of them, they were Morgan's men. They were clearly keeping an eye on the saloons along the street, checking on every cowhand who entered or left. Here and there, the yellow beam of a kerosene lamp shone through a shop window and the still air held the faintly discernible odour of oil burning in other lamps.

Keeping his head averted, he rode past the men. At any moment, he expected to hear a harsh yell which would tell him that he had been recognized, but it never came. He reached the far end of the main street and turned sharp left, into a dark alley. He could hear shouting and yelling back there in the street. A couple of shots were fired and the clump of running feet on the boardwalks were clearly audible as others ran to see the cause for this new excitement.

Vance tensed, then relaxed as the thought struck him that perhaps other eyes had seen him riding into town, more friendly eyes, and this diversion had been deliberately engineered by Doc Manton. Slowly, he rode along the narrow alley, the sound of his horse's hoofs ringing metallically on the stone.

He thought he saw a sudden movement in the pitch-black shadows at the end of the alley, but he couldn't be sure until a voice hissed out of the darkness: 'Vance? Over here.'

He edged the horse in towards the wall of the tall grain-house, dropped from the saddle. As his eyes grew accustomed to the darkness, he saw the shapes of other horses around him and of men standing in little, quiet groups.

Most of them carried rifles in their hands or had gunbelts slung about their middles. Doc Manton came forward.

'Glad you got here, Vance,' he said tightly. 'I got the men together like I promised. 'Twenty-eight, all with guns and ready to use 'em.'

'Did you bring along Marty Benson?'

'Sure. Got him here too. Didn't want to ride with us, but we managed to persuade him after a little talk. Got the idea he wanted to go to Morgan, but we talked him out of that.' The other uttered a low, harsh laugh and Vance could guess what methods had been used to prevent Benson from talking. He eyed the rest of the men critically. There was nothing to show from their faces that the thought of the fighting ahead was churning at their insides, as it undoubtedly was.

'There are three of Morgan's men outside the sheriff's office, spotted them on my way in. They're watching the town, looking for any sign of trouble. The rest of the men will be out with Devlin and that hell-cat of a daughter of Morgan's. They know we're building up some kind of a plan against them, but they aren't sure of what we intend to do or where we're going to strike. They may be watching all trails out of town, particularly into the Badlands, but I'm figuring on them expecting us to stay here until morning and ride out in daylight, when we'd stand a better chance of finding that gang's hideout. If we ride through the night and hit them by dawn, we stand a good chance of taking them before they're ready for trouble.'

'We're ready to ride out whenever you give the word, Vance,' said Manton tightly. 'Want to have a word with Benson first? Guess we'd better make sure he knows why we're bringing him along and that we'll stand for no nonsense once we're out there. He thinks too much of his hide not to be scared of Hagberg, even with us backing him up.'

'Let me have a talk with him,' suggested Vance. He threw a swift glance up at the sky over his head. There were only a few stars and several large areas of dark clouds were building up, blotting out the few which still shone clearly, one by one. He gave a nod of satisfaction to himself. At least it would prevent moonlight from giving them away. He glanced round as two men came up with the struggling figure of Benson between them. They pushed him forward in front of Vance.

'What d'yuh want with me, mister?' whined the other piteously. 'I told you before in the saloon when you started asking me questions, that I knew nothing about the whereabouts of the Hagberg gang. I still tell you, I don't know.'

'Sure, I've heard all of that before.' Vance's tone was deliberately harsh. 'But I know that you're lying. I've been having quite a nice little talk with Morgan and his daughter a little while ago, and from what they told me, you know a lot that you haven't told us. I'm not saying that you're working hand in hand with those gunslammers, but you sure know where they have their hideout. And what's more, you're going to lead us to it. If you don't, then I'll have you arrested and taken back to Dodge for obstructing the law and conspiracy with these outlaws, and believe me, I can make that charge stick if I've a mind to.'

'Mister, there's a lot happening in this territory that you don't know nuthin' about. If you reckon that you can beat the Hagberg gang with this posse, then you're mistaken – and to be mistaken about a thing like that means to be dead.'

'Don't be too sure about that,' Vance warned him quietly, purposefully. 'These men have guns and they'll shoot. They've taken too much from these gunslingers and now that they've got the chance, they intend to put an end to it. All we're asking you to do is lead us there. If you're scared of being hit, then you can get back here and we'll do the rest.'

'This ain't my fight,' protested the other hoarsely, his long face contorted. 'I'm a prospector. These men ain't done anything to me.'

Deliberately, Vance pulled his gun from its holster and drew it on the other man, his face tight and fixed. 'Get on to that horse they've brought along for you,' he said ominously, 'and ride. You'll tell us what we want to know, or I'll shoot you.' He spoke as though he meant it, wondering if the other would realize that he was only bluffing. For a moment, the old prospector paused, then he shrugged, defeated, turned and walked back to the horse which stood waiting near the wall. Heaving a sigh of relief, Vance holstered the gun and turned to Manton. 'Let's ride, Doc,' he said harshly. 'We've no time to waste.'

'Don't blame him,' said the other as he swung himself into the saddle. 'He's scared of what's going to happen.'

'Sure he's scared,' retorted Vance. 'We're all scared. It's no sin being scared at a time like this. The sin is in running away like yellow-striped skunks.'

He headed his mount slowly along the alley towards the far edge of town, the others close on his heels, dark shadows of vengeance in the night.

5

Guns to the South

They made it out of town without arousing any suspicion, walking their horses most of the way until they were well clear and in open country. Glancing sideways out of the corner of his eyes, Vance saw that the men were in a quiet, but savage, mood. This had been building up for a long time and now they were taking matters into their own hands, doing something to rid the land of these gunslamming parasites who were ruining the territory, besides keeping every decent family there in a state of fear and apprehension. He wondered how many times in the past they had tried to get the sheriff to take matters in hand, to get a posse together and ride out into the Badlands after the Hagberg gang, before they had been disillusioned, finding that he was in the pay of Morgan, the big cattle-boss. A couple of miles out of Big Wheel, they touched spurs to their horses, set them at a gallop and made good progress, no longer afraid to make noise. Any of Morgan's men out scouting the surrounding hills for Vance might pick up the sound of their hoofs, but he anticipated no move from these ranch hands. It was even likely that Morgan had given orders that the vigilantes were to be allowed to ride through into the Badlands unmolested, thereby hoping that between them, both they and Hagberg's outlaw band might be wiped out, leaving the town wide open for him to ride in and take over without any opposition.

Vance compressed his lips tightly as the thought crossed his mind. He was determined, more than ever, that Morgan and his men were also to be rounded up after he had dealt with Hagberg. Beside him, Doc Manton rode tall and grim in the saddle. Vance smiled a little as he contemplated the other for a moment. It was impossible to make an accurate estimate of the other's age, but he figured that the other was close on sixty; yet here he was, riding out with the others, filled with a zeal and a determination to shoot it out with these outlaws.

As though conscious of Vance's gaze on him, the older man turned, gave him a tight sort of grin. 'Never figured I'd be riding the trail like this with a Texas Ranger, heading into big trouble,' he declared quietly. He threw a dark glance over the other men riding with them. 'Wonder how many of them will fight when they come up against these killers?'

'So long as most of them stand their ground, we should make out fine,' said Vance. 'I ain't worried so much about Benson. Once he leads us to their hideout, I'll be satisfied.'

'You ain't scared he might turn and head back to Big Wheel to warn Morgan?'

Vance pursed his lips. 'Reckon he could do that. But I figure Morgan will know where we are soon enough, and he'll have figured that once we deal with Hagberg, those of us that are left will be gunning for him.'

Doc Manton asked: 'You're going to ask these men to ride right back into town and deal with Morgan the minute they've finished here?'

'I've got to. I know what Morgan's plan is. He reckons that he can ride in and take over Big Wheel while we're occupied out here. We've got to drive him out before he has time to make any preparations.'

'All right, Ranger. I'll see that the men follow you back to town as soon as we've flushed this bunch of rats out of their nest.'

Overhead, a storm was gathering, the dark clouds swirling up from the horizon. The wind was rising too, blowing off the Badlands, swirling about them, plucking at them with harsh fingers. In a way, it helped, riding through the storm. The wind would deaden the thunder of their hoofs and the Hagberg gang would not be expecting them to ride in a night such as this.

The full fury of the storm hit them as they left the prairie and swung off the main trail, hitting out into the desert to the south The wind whipped the sand into their faces, smothering them in a whirling, yellow blanket, the myriad grains working their way into the folds of their skin, into their eyes and nostrils. After an hour of riding through the tumult, Vance would not have been surprised if half of the men had decided to turn back for town. He could scarcely have found it in his heart to have blamed them, but they kept on riding, their heads bowed, their hats pulled well down over their eyes to shield their faces from the gathering madness of the storm. Out here, in the Badlands, it had been known for a storm like this to madden horses, whipping them into a tempestuous fury so that they became uncontrollable. In the past a few trail bosses had tried to bring a herd of cattle across these lands, seeking a shorter trail to the north and east, but they had been forced to yield to the fury of nature. These were crazy lands in which it was almost impossible for a man to survive.

The wind died a little as they reached the mountain trail and began to climb above the level of the desert. The sand now lay below them and although the wind still had sufficient force in it to make a man ride low in the saddle, there was no longer those irritating, tortuous grains of sand scattering against them from all sides.

Now and again, Vance rode up beside Marty Benson, edging his mount close to the other, yelling at the top of his voice to make himself heard above the insane shrieking of the wind.

'You're sure that we're on the right trial, Benson? If you're thinking of double-crossing us and leading us into the mountains on a wild goose chase, you'd better change your mind – and quick.'

'I said I'd take you there,' shouted the other. 'If you're all so set on getting yourselves killed, that's your business. But I don't aim to stick around once you meet up with those outlaws.'

'Just you lead us to 'em and we'll do the rest,' promised Vance. He leaned forward in the saddle and tried to peer through narrowed eyes into the darkness. It still wanted three hours or so to dawn and by that time, he hoped to have most of his men in position, ready to take the outlaws by surprise.

An hour later, the wind died down abruptly as if somebody had shut off a tap. They rode in single file over a hump-backed ridge, then around the face of the mountain, edging their nervous horses forward slowly, in places where a wrong step could mean instant death as man and mount slipped over the edge of the trail and went plunging down into the fissure.

There was little said on that long ride into the Badlands. The men were hard-faced and stony-eyed, their nostrils pinched and white after the lashing of the storm, their minds too full of what lay ahead of them for any conversation. Some fingered their rifles absently, others stared straight ahead as if trying to pierce the darkness and the distance and make out the outlaws, where they lay in their hideout somewhere ahead in the rocks.

Once they reached the end of the trail which wound around the rock and reached the long, valley floor, they did not spare their horses. There were still a couple or so hours of darkness left to them and, according to Benson, a lot of distance to cover. More and more, Vance had the uneasy feeling that the old prospector was keeping something back from him, that he knew a little more than he had told. But he pushed that thought out of his mind as he rode. So long as the other led them to the outlaws and they caught the whole bunch, he could worry about that later.

Benson, in the lead, held up his right hand just as dawn was beginning to break. The column came to a halt and Vance, with Doc Manton beside him, rode up to the old-timer.

'This the place?' asked Vance sharply. He looked about him. In front of them, the buttes stretched away almost as far as the eye could see. To their right, a narrow, dimly-seen trail led up into the bare, scrub-dotted hills which rose up at the foot of the tall mountains. Even though he could see nothing, Vance felt an itch between his shoulder blades, the old soldier's uneasiness for an ambush he could feel but could not see. He ran his gaze swiftly over the distant canyon wall, probing the eroded sandstone face of it, and the covering of old cedars and brush near the top.

'That's where they have their hideout,' said the other tonelessly. He rubbed at the bristles on his face and made a scratching sound with the back of his hand. 'I seen 'em go in there and come out plenty of times during the past year or so. I've never ventured in there myself. Ain't healthy to do anything like that. But I don't reckon they'll be far in there. Plenty of places, old mine workings where they can hide out. Used to be a few drilling installations there too, years back. It's as good a place as any to hide, I suppose.'

Vance nodded tersely. He continued to search the broken boulders and the smooth sandstone of the wall in the dim light of dawn until he sighted what he was looking for. A split in the rocky wall about a quarter of a mile away, just about the point where that narrow trail disappeared into the face of the canyon, formed a thin shaft of colour where there was undoubtedly an opening between split boulders.

'We'll head up there and take a look-see,' he ordered. Glancing at the prospector, he said sharply: 'You coming with us, Benson? We need every gun we can get on our side. But I want nobody up there with me who'll turn and run at the first shot.'

The other debated the question for a moment, then shook his head slowly. 'Reckon I'll stay down here, Ranger, just in case they head this way.'

Vance almost smiled at the other's excuse, then turned swiftly in the saddle and motioned the rest of the men forward. They rode slowly now that they were so close to their objective, their horses soft-footing it across the smooth sand. Reaching the bottom of the canyon wall, he urged his mount forward, pulling tightly on the reins up the rocky, ride-cut rise. Here, the trail was almost completely obliterated in places, but, glancing down, his keen, trailsman's gaze noticed signs which pointed to the fact that men on horseback had been along this way several times, and recently. Clearly, the old prospector was telling the truth when he had claimed to have seen the outlaws heading in this direction. It was wild country that lay up ahead, ideal for defence, and this was obviously the reason why it had been chosen. He wondered if they had a lookout posted on top of one of the highest ridges. If they had, and it seemed an excellent precaution, unless they were so confident that they would not be attacked at dawn, the man would have spotted them while they were still many miles away.

But there was no time to worry about that now. They had committed themselves and if they found the gang waiting for them, they would have to fight it out, without the advantage of surprise. Clem Hagberg was an old Confederate officer, and in spite of the fact that he had been dismissed from his regiment ignominiously, he would still know sufficient of military tactics to have disposed his men to their best advantage.

There was not much space within the opening. Vance led the way, gently urging his mount through, eyes flicking from side to side. The place was too silent for his liking and it held a waiting quality over it which increased the feeling of uneasiness in his mind. His horse stumbled over loose rocks and judging from the sound behind him, the softly muttered curses of the men, he gathered that they were having just as much trouble with their horses.

Here, they were shielded by rock and boulders from the trail below and even though he turned his head, he could no longer see the solitary figure on horseback where Marty Benson sat in the wide stretch of desert, afraid to join them in their fight, but apparently equally afraid to wheel his horse and make the long ride back to town.

Twenty yards further on, the canyon widened out in front of them and the old mine workings of which Benson had talked lay spread out in front of them. At some time in the past, silver or gold must have been found out here in the mountains, and a veritable army of prospectors had moved in, throwing up their wooden shacks in this valley, hidden away from the outside world by the high ridges and canyons.

Most of the wooden shacks had collapsed over the years and stood with whole walls and roofs fallen in. But here and there, Vance's gaze took in several others which seemed to have been repaired quite recently using timber taken from the rest. That alone told him that this was the lair of the outlaws. The place seemed to be deserted. But that was, he knew, only an outward impression. In his mind's eye, he could visualize the men inside those clustered shacks, rifles ready, aimed in their direction, waiting for them to come out into the open.

Vance loosened his sixes, then motioned to the men with the rifles to move forward, leaving their horses at the head of the canyon. With their longer range, they would be able to lay a devastating fire on the shacks. He waited impatiently as the men slid into rocks, rifles ready. Others moved along the rocky ledges, until the entire area had been surrounded. That was one point these outlaws had apparently, foolishly, overlooked when they had holed themselves up here, he reflected. If they had decided to make a fight of it at the canyon mouth, they could have held off an army. But now, they had left it a little too late and it had been comparatively easy to surround them completely.

When he estimated that all of the men were in position, he touched spurs to his mount and rode forward, into the open, eyes alert, ready to whip his body to one side at the first hint of trouble.

'Are you in there, Hagberg?' he yelled loudly. His voice echoed and re-echoed from the rocky ledges on all sides of him. From somewhere near the old mine working he thought he heard the snicker of a horse, but he couldn't be sure.

Then something moved at the back of one of the windows. He saw it out of the corner of his eye, the glint of sunlight on the steel of a rifle barrel as it was thrust through the opening. Swiftly, automatic reflexes threw his body sideways in the saddle as he galvanized himself into motion. The bullet hummed through the air where his head had been a split second earlier and ricocheted off the hard rock at his back. Even as he pulled his guns, he heard a loud voice shout:

'I don't know how you managed to trail us to this place, but you'll never get out of here alive. I've got twenty men with me just in case you're figuring on shooting it out with me. Reckon you'll be the fourth Ranger they decided to send in after me. Well, you've had a mite more luck than the other three, but this is where it comes to an end.'

Obviously the outlaws had been taken completely by surprise. They had not expected anyone to be so fool-hardy as to try to make the mountain trail in pitch darkness and with a storm like that which had blown up during the night. Probably they had figured that any attack would come later in the day. Now they were unprepared and from Hagberg's words, they seemed to think that he was all alone. Well, they'd soon discover how wrong that was, he thought grimly.

More rifle shots hammered from the windows of the shacks as he flung himself out of the saddle, hitting the rock hard before coming up on to his knees, throwing lead.

'You don't stand a chance, Hagberg,' he yelled. 'This whole place is surrounded. Throw down your guns and come out with your hands up. I'll see that you all get a fair trial back in Dodge.'

Hagberg laughed harshly. 'If you're figuring on taking any of us back, Ranger, you're welcome to come and take your chance. I suppose you've got a handful of those damned vigilantes from Big Wheel at the back of you, otherwise you wouldn't be so big with your threats. They ain't going to worry me none.'

'I don't intend to warn you again, Hagberg.' He kept his tone even. 'You killed those three Rangers and you'll hang for that if you're taken alive. That goes for most of your men too.'

'Then we don't have any choice, do we?' sneered the other. He seemed to be keeping himself well hidden behind one of the windows, and as he lay there among the rocks, Vance tried to figure out which one it was, but the echoes which rang along the wide valley made it impossible to trace the sound.

Rifle shots barked out from the rocks all around the clearing as the men opened fire. Someone cried out gruffly from one of the shacks as a bullet found its mark. Swiftly, Vance fired at the nearest of the shacks from which return fire was coming. He could see the red flashes from the rifle muzzles as the outlaws thrust them through the windows, loosed off a couple of shots, then ducked back in again. A man lying among the rocks near Vance suddenly yelled, rolled over on to his side and pressed his hand to his shoulder. The blood was beginning to well slowly from the bullet wound, squeezing its way through his tightly clenched fingers. His face twisted in a spasm of pain. Swiftly, Vance wriggled over to him. 'Just lie back and keep your head down,' he cautioned quickly. 'It's just a flesh wound. We'll take that slug out as soon as this is over. Think you can stay there?'

The other twisted his lips into a thin grimace. 'Reckon I ain't going no place from here, Ranger,' he said tightly.

'Good man.' Vance glanced up, cast swiftly about him, then motioned towards Doc Manton. The other came crawling over quickly.

'This man's been hit in the shoulder, Doc. See if you can do anything for him at the moment. In the meantime, I'm going to try to get up to that shack out there. If we can smoke 'em out of one ranch, we can move in and take the others one at a time. There'd be too many casualties if we tried to rush 'em from both sides.'

'You'll never make it,' said the other tightly. 'There are at least twenty yards of open ground to cover before you get anywhere near that shack and they'll be shooting at you all the way.'

'I'll get everyone else to cover me,' he argued. 'Besides, it's our only chance. We could stay here in the rocks all day and just waste ammunition. They could have plenty stacked away in there and they've only to wait until we run out before rushing us.'

Without waiting for the other to reply, he edged his way forward until he was up with the foremost line of men still crouched behind the barrier of rocks. He gave them urgent orders, outlining his plan to them. They nodded quickly to show that they agreed.

One man said quietly: 'That cottonwood tree next to the shack. It's the biggest I've seen in these parts. I reckon those branches could take a man's weight quite easily and one of them overhangs the roof for quite a distance.' He inclined his head in the direction of the shack.

Vance narrowed his eyes and gave a quick nod. 'That's a pretty good idea. A man could easily drop on to that roof and do a deal of damage before they could get at him.' He rubbed his chin thoughtfully as the idea formed in his mind. Then he reached a sudden decision. 'Get ready to cover me, boys,' he said tersely. 'As soon as I get close to that tree, blast the other shacks with everything you've got. There won't be much to fear from the men in that particular cabin.'

He went down on to his belly, slithered forward like a snake among the rocks and gullies which led towards the nearest shack. Several bullets whined and screeched over his head as he wriggled forward, but most of them were strays and not deliberately aimed in his direction. He paused as he reached the end of his cover. In front of him there was an open space of nearly fifty yards between his rocky cover and the shack itself. In this vast area, not a single bush or shrub grew to give him any protection. He sucked in a deep breath, plucked his guns from their holsters, and thrust himself out into the open. In the same instant, someone yelled something behind him and every gun on that side of the canyon opened up, blasting at the other shacks, keeping the outlaws under cover, forcing them to crouch down behind their windows, giving them no chance to raise their heads and fire at him as he ran, weaving from side to side to present the smallest possible target.

The sound of gunfire filled the crisp, clear air in the canyon. Two windows suddenly shattered along the front of the shack. He saw the barrels of rifles being poked through, aimed in his direction as the defenders spotted him and guessed his intentions. Leaping and twisting, he flung himself forward expecting to feel the hot, searing touch of a leaden slug in his chest every moment. But he seemed to bear a charmed life Nothing touched him as he raced forward, reached the side of the shack, and crouched, gasping, against the dry timber which had been piled up outside. For a moment, he deliberated on the wisdom of merely setting fire to the shack and burning the outlaws out of it, then decided against it. Under cover of a pillar of smoke, it would be possible for the rest of the gunslingers to make it to their hidden horses unseen and ride out of the canyon. Whatever happened, they had to finish this here and now.

Pausing only to regain his wind, he eased the guns into his holsters and began to climb, pulling himself up the tree hand over hand. It was more difficult than he had anticipated and there was the added danger of being hit by a stray bullet from the guns of the vigilantes firing from the rocks. It needed one man to be a trifle over-excited with his aim, and he was finished.

A shot cracked out from one of the other shacks and the bullet smashed along the branch and snapped twigs over his head as it screamed by. He kept his head as long as possible as he eased his way along the overhanging branch which lay across the roof of the shack. A two-foot drop and he was on the roof itself, jerking the Colts from their holsters, tip-toeing catlike across the narrow, slanted roof. He could hear voices below him, inside the shack. The men in there had an idea where he was and were pondering what to do about it. He heard one of them give a roar of savage anger and an instant later, there was a sound immediately below him and the head of a bull-necked man appeared in the opening of the window. Vance wasted no time. Without compunction, he shot the man in the head and then withdrew out of sight. Under normal conditions, he might have been ready to take most of these outlaws alive. Whether functioning as a lawman or a human being, he was not the type to kill purely for the sake of killing. But this was different. These were the men who had shot the other three Rangers in cold blood and that was something he could never forget. Something cold and inhuman seemed to take hold of him, to force him along, to make him oblivious to everything else but the need to kill so that a lot of good people might remain alive.

He fired instinctively at every target that presented itself and gradually, the volume of fire from the shack beneath him dwindled until only a desultory shot was fired. Dropping from the roof, he hit the ground with a jar that shook him to his teeth, then kicked in the door of the shack and burst inside, the guns in his hands. His eyes took in everything in a wide, unfocused glance. The four men lying on the filthy floor by the windows, one of them the bull-necked man he had shot from the roof. And the man standing near the stove, his left arm hanging limp and useless where a slug had torn into his shoulder, but with a gun still clutched tightly in his right and a murderous look on his heavily-jowled face.

'This is where you get it, Ranger,' he snarled, bringing up the barrel of the gun until it was lined up on Vance's chest. In that split second, Vance fired, he fired instinctively, knowing that he had only a bare fraction of a second in which to beat the other. As his gun roared in his hand, a sudden took of stupefied astonishment spread over the other man's swarthy features. The muscles of his jaw seemed to slacken and something fled from his narrowed eyes as if a light had been switched off at the back of them. Then he pitched forward, the slug from his gun tearing into the floor at his feet.

He turned each of the other bodies over with the toe of his boot, then went to the door and signalled to the men in the rocks. They came rushing forward in a loose bunch, spurred on more by fear than anything else. One man was shot as he stumbled among the rocks. but even as he staggered and fell, someone caught him by the arm and dragged him forward into the shelter of the shack. Outside, the rest of the men were still firing.

'Get that wounded man over by the wall,' ordered

Vance, 'away from the windows, and one of you see what you can do for him.'

There was still plenty of highly accurate fire from the other outlaws, bunched together in three other shacks. Swiftly, Vance crammed shells into the empty chambers of his Colts. He came back into the fire from one of the windows, just as one man hurled his last shot. Cautiously, he lifted his head until he was able to see the other shacks. He could see more of the vigilantes snaking forward from the rear positions, throwing lead as they advanced. This was what Vance had been wating for. Swiftly, he called the men together, led them out into the open, firing as they ran. A slug hit the side of one of the broken-down cabins, ricocheted off and laid a red-hot bar along his left arm. Then they reached the next shack and the door burst open, and one of the outlaws came staggering out with blood on his shirt. His face was a dirty grey behind the unkempt beard, but he gave a roar of defiance and began hurling lead from both sixes. There was a sudden tensed feeling inside Vance's body as he leapt to one side and pressed the triggers of his own guns, as if there had been a steel spring inside him, coiled and tight, ready to unwind.

He fired instinctively even as he went to one side, going down into a half crouch. The man dropped on to his face, still pulling up his guns as he fell. Swiftly Vance jumped over his inert body and leapt inside the shack, guns spitting flame in all directions. Two men, standing at the windows, turned quickly, but never had a chance against this human tornado. Savagely, he cut them down with two shots, turning over each man, staring down into the dead faces. So far, he had seen no sign of Clem Hagberg, the man he wanted above all of the others, the undisputed leader of this cut-throat gang. Whatever happened, he must not be allowed to get away.

Outside, the fury of the gun battle was diminishing slowly as the remaining outlaws were overrun by the vigilantes. These men from Big Wheel had fought as Vance had never expected them to fight. A few had clearly served in the Civil War and knew how to handle both themselves and their weapons, but the others were storekeepers or bartenders, ordinary townsfolk who had scarcely ever handled a weapon in anger. But they were now angry and determined men. Angry at what had happened in the past and determined that this blot on the territory must be wiped clean.

Less than half an hour later, it was all over. Incredibly, they had won. Three of the Hagberg gang had surrendered when they had seen that they stood no chance of winning. The others were either dead or badly wounded in the shacks, or lying among the cottonwoods in the open. Vance went round them one by one. When he had finished this chore, he knew with a sick certainty that Clem Hagberg, the man whose picture he had seen on the wanted posters back in Dodge, was not among the men there. He bit his lip in angry mortification and went to find Doc Manton.

'Any sign of Hagberg himself?' he asked tensely.

The other shook his head. 'None. Figured you might have met up with him and taken care of him personally.'

'Then he must either have managed to slip through our fingers, or he's still holed up somewhere in the area. Possibly in one of those old, abandoned workings.' Vance rubbed the back of his hand over his eyes. The sun had risen now and the heat waves were reflected from the yellow sand in dizzying spirals that hurt the eyes, forcing their way into his brain, even though he closed his eyes momentarily.

'If he's in there,' Manton jerked his hand in the direction of the workings which led down into the bowels of the rearing canyon face, 'then you'll never find him. There could be an ideal escape route leading through there, out to some place in the desert to the north of here. He could have slipped out the minute he saw that things were going against him and he'll be miles away by now.'

Reluctantly, Vance was forced to acknowledge that the other was, in all probability, right. Hagberg was no fool. He must have foreseen that there might come a day when the law would catch up with him, even out here, and he had laid his escape plans accordingly. He cursed himself for not having foreseen such a possibility earlier. Then there might have been time to go after him.

He walked over to where the three prisoners were seated in the shadow of the towering rocks and stood for a moment, staring down at them, a tight grin on his lips. He said harshly: 'Any of you men know where Hagberg is right now? It might mean that you'll go to State prison rather than be strung up, if you talk now.'

They remained silent, staring at the ground at their feet. For a moment, Vance was silent also. Then he caught the nearest man by the shirt, bunching the material in his fingers and hauling him to his feet. 'Answer me when I speak to you,' he said thinly, his lips drawn back. 'Where's Hagberg?'

'He slipped away into the tunnel back there,' grunted the other gruffly.

'Long ago?' demanded the Ranger tightly. He did not release his hold on the other's shirt.

'Long enough,' retorted the man. 'You'll never catch up with him now.'

'Does that tunnel out there lead anywhere?'

The man moistened his lips with the tip of his tongue, then nodded his head as Vance tightened his grip, hauling him close. 'Yeah, out into the desert, about three miles north of here. He had a horse in the tunnel, ready to get away, as soon as the fighting started.'

Angrily, Vance thrust the other from him so that he fell between his two companions. Doc Manton said quietly 'That's what I feared all the time. He'd leave his men here to die if necessary so long as he could make his getaway.'

There was a far-away look in Vance's eyes as he nodded. 'I've an idea, though, that I know where he'll be headed for right this minute. If I'm right, then we ought to be able to catch up with him, long before he can slip to safety over the Mexican border.'

'How can you be sure that you know what he'll do?' asked the other.

'It's quite simple. He'll know that someone has led us here. We would never have discovered this place ourselves. And as far as he knows, there are only a small handful of people who know the whereabouts of these workings. Fewer still who know that this is their hideout.'

'You figure he's gone after Benson, down there in the desert?'

Vance shook his head emphatically. 'He wouldn't waste his time on that old soak. No, he'll figure that either Devlin or Carla Morgan told us about this place and that whoever it was, did it for the purpose of getting him out of the way, and having a clear trail for owning all of this territory.'

'Makes sense,' agreed the other. 'You heading back for the Morgan ranch?'

Vance gave a quick nod. 'If I'm right, Hagberg will be there, seeking revenge, If not, we may still be able to stop Morgan before he rides out into Big Wheel, hoping to take over the town.'

'I'll get the rest of the men together and we'll ride out.' The other was all action now. He had tasted his first battle, had drawn blood. and was anxious to draw some more.

Most of the men were feeling the same way. Almost all of them were elated at having destroyed this terrible menace which had hung over them for the best part of two years. Previously, they had regarded Hagberg and his bunch of killers as something which they could never hope to fight. Now, they had come out with this Ranger and they had beaten this gang on their own ground. They were still feeling in the mood for more fighting and Vance knew better than to stop them. This was the time to let them fight, while the excited, anticipatory feeling was still there, while they still possessed that rare confidence in themselves which had been lacking before.

They fired the shacks in the canyon before riding back along the narrow, winding trail. Benson was still there in the desert, waiting for them and Vance could see him casting anxious eyes towards the black smoke that curled up lazily in a huge pall over the mountain. He watched the three prisoners closely as they were herded by, with two men carrying rifles on either side of them, their hands bound and tied to the pommels of their saddles.

'I see you found 'em,' he said, looking directly at Vance as he spoke.

Doc Manton said tersely: 'With small help from you, Benson.'

'I brung you out here, didn't I?' protested the other, the whining edge still apparent in his voice.

'And that's all you did, you drunken old reprobate,' declared the Doc. 'We lost three good men and five have been injured.'

'Didn't I say that they would give you a fight of it?'

'You did,' muttered Vance. 'Now get riding. Mebbe next time you'll pitch in and give us a hand.'

'Sure, sure,' said the other affably.

'Good. Because we're heading for the Morgan ranch, where we expect that we'll find not only Morgan and his men, but Clem Hagberg too. He slipped away from us through the mine workings in the mountain, had a horse there.'

'Then you didn't kill Hagberg?' There was the unmistakable glint of fear in the little man's eyes now and Vance almost felt sorry for him. Then he jigged his horse and rode away, taking the lead as they formed into single column to pass through the hills.

The faint smudge of grey smoke still painted the sky by the time they reached the main trail leading into Big Wheel, and cut across it, heading north-east. As they rode, Vance had the feeling that perhaps now his mission was nearly over. He had accomplished most of what he had set out to do. Vengeance, in some part, had been claimed for the deaths of his three Ranger companions. But now, he knew that he would not stop until he had helped to clear this entire territory of killers and crooks, and brought law and order to Big Wheel.

There was now a sudden icy coldness in Vance's brain which washed away every other emotion that had ever been there. The men who rode with him stared straight ahead of them, features tight and fixed, eyes bright with the battle light. Even Doc Manton rode tall in the saddle now, carrying his sixty years like a twenty-year-old out with his first posse.

They rode through the dry, parched scrubland, before they came to the boundary fence beyond which lay the lush green, well-watered grass and the grazing herds of beef which were Morgan's pride. Vance paused only for a moment at the fence, then motioned a couple of the men forward. Lassooing the posts, they tied the ropes to their saddles, urged their mounts to pull. The strong ropes tautened, quivered a little with the strain which was being placed on them. Then the posts were uprooted and the large section of wire had been pulled clear of the line.

They rode through on to the Morgan spread. The tightness was beginning to grow again in Vance's body. He found himself sliding his sixes up and down in their holsters absently as he rodded the horse. They had ridden many miles since the previous night when they had left Big Wheel and their horses were beginning to tire. The storm of the night before and the tremendous heat of the desert was beginning to take its toll.

When they finally topped the long, low rise which overlooked the ranch, Vance reined his mount and let it blow, leaning forward in the saddle, resting his arms over the pommel. A thin column of black smoke curled up from the ranch, but that was the only sign of life. No sign of any horses tethered either at the hitching post in front of the ranch, or in the corral. Vance narrowed his eyes and puckered his brow in sudden thought. It certainly looked from there as though they had arrived too late, as if Morgan, in spite of his wound, had decided to go into Big Wheel, take over the town and make his last, glorious stand there against the forces of the law and order which he had so often despised in the past. It was possible also that Devlin and Carla were with him, ready to fight rather than to submit to the people of Big Wheel.

6

Desperado

When it was obvious that, somehow, the vigilantes had gained the upper hand and there was little chance of his men holding them off for any length of time, Clem Hagberg decided that only one course now lay open to him. Sooner or later, he had anticipated that the law would catch up with him. Even having killed those three Rangers sent to capture him had failed to secure any lasting sense of power for him in this territory. But he had planned his getaway route carefully and well against a time such as this.

Gunfire was still thundering along the canyon as he darted from the rear of the cabin in which he had been crouching behind the window, and ran, half doubled, towards the old mine workings set in the face of the canyon. A few shots hurried past him as he ran, but he did not seem to have been seen by any of the vigilantes. The horse which was tethered just inside the tunnel leading through the solid rock was the best of the bunch. A fleet animal with plenty of staying power, and one which he had chosen deliberately for a time like this.

He had just reached the entrance and was on the point of moving into the darkness of the tunnel, ready to throw his saddle on to the mount, when the sudden movement behind him caught his attention. Swiftly, he whirled, gun sighing from its holster. A dark figure had detached itself from one of the shacks and was running urgently in his direction. He eased himself to one side, his back hard against the canyon wall, head back, eyes narrowed as he waited for the other to come closer. If this were the Ranger, he might get his revenge, even now, he figured. It would be easy to shoot him down as he came into the workings; just as easy as it had been to kill those other three, shooting them all in the back from ambush.

Boots clattered loudly on the rusted rails which led down into the mountain. Whoever it was, he reflected tightly, he was pretty sure of himself, or else it was fear that was driving him on. His lips tightened into a hard, grim line. The other men knew of this getaway route. Perhaps one of them had decided to try to make a break for it, thinking that he had been killed in the shooting.

The man swung swiftly around the corner, came to a sudden halt as Hagberg stepped away from the wall, his gun levelled on the other's chest.

'So, it's you, Utter,' he snarled. I might have figured you would come running after me. No doubt hoping to find that I'd been shot back there leaving this way open for you. Sorry to have to disappoint you like this, but there's only one horse and I'm taking him. I can't have anyone else on my trail who might give me away to that Ranger out there. You'll have to stay here and take your chance with him and those vigilantes he's brought with him.'

'But you ain't going to shoot me down like this,' said the other hoarsely. The muscles of his face were working convulsively under the skin which had been burned by the sun to the colour of old leather. 'We could both make it easy on that horse. They don't know about this tunnel, or where it leads. We could both be away and over the border long before they knew we'd escaped.'

Hagberg smiled, but it was not a nice smile and never

reached his eyes. His finger tightened on the trigger of his gun until the whiteness showed under the skin. 'You've been a good man in the past, Utter,' he said silkily, 'but the trouble is that I don't aim to head for the border until I'm good and ready. There's some business I have to take care of before I run out and shake the dust of this state off my boots. Somebody double-crossed us and gave away our hideout to that Ranger. I reckon I know who it was and they're going to have to pay. Before I'm finished with them, they'll wish they'd never been born. I'll have them pleading with me to kill them.'

'Then you'll need help. What if something goes wrong and they're waiting for you, expecting you to turn up?'

Hagberg shook his head. The other must have seen the look of finality in the outlaw leader's eyes for he made one last despairing effort, and went for his guns, throwing himself sideways against the far wall of the tunnel entrance as he did so. He had the guns half-way out of their holsters, when Hagberg's bullets cut him down. Slowly, almost reluctantly, his body slumped against the eroded sandstone, his legs sliding from beneath him as though no longer able to bear his weight. His eyes glazed over and his hands relaxed, fingers opening as they loosed their hold on the handles of the guns. With a final, swiftly appraising glance in the direction of the shacks in the centre of the canyon floor, Hagberg turned and ran to where the horse stood tethered to the stake driven deeply into the ground. Throwing the saddle over it, he tightened the cinch, rammed fresh slugs into the guns, then climbed up into the saddle and urged the horse forward, into the stretching river of darkness that lay in front of him.

The tunnel had been driven deep through the mountain back in the days before the war when there had been plenty of rich silver veins in this sandstone and the prospectors and get-rich-quick men from the east had arrived in flocks, seeking to make their fortune. Several had done so and had gone back to the east, far richer than when they had arrived. Others had spent their silver in the saloons in Big Wheel and the other towns which had sprung up almost overnight in the neighbourhood. That was when men like McCord and Morgan had made their pile, when they had swindled most of these men out of their land grants, taken over the mines lock, stock and barrel and then, when the seams had run out, had converted all of their cash into the purchase of vast tracts of prairie, setting up the huge beef herds.

It was a treacherous trail through the heart of the mountain with no light to show the way, but he had made this journey several times in the past and knew most of the way by heart. Besides, there was plenty of time. The men he had deserted would continue to fight until their last bullet, their last drop of blood, for they were in this as deep as he was, and only a hanging lay at the end of it for all of them. He had chosen his men carefully when he had built up this outlaw band. Men whose records in half a dozen states were such that they could never double-cross him without putting a noose around their own necks. Now that policy of his was beginning to pay definite dividends. They would hold off those vigilantes long enough for him to get clean away. Once he came out of the mountain, into the stretch of desert to the north, he would head for Morgan's ranch and have it out with his foreman and that she-devil of a daughter of his. He did not doubt that the two of them had been instrumental in giving that Ranger all of the information he needed to track him down to his lair in the Badlands. But no one went against Clem Hagberg and got away with it. He gritted his teeth as a sharp flood of anger poured momentarily through him. Then he forced himself to relax. There would be a time of reckoning as far as they were concerned. Also, he knew that Devlin had been paying many of the men on the Morgan payroll a double salary out of his own money so that they would obey his orders when the time came for a showdown with Morgan. He thought he knew a way whereby he could turn this to his own advantage, take over those men himself, once he had killed Devlin and tamed that she-devil. He composed himself with these thoughts as he gave the horse its head and allowed it to find its own pace in the darkness.

Water dripped continually down the walls of the tunnel here in the very heart of the mountain. Up there, on the surface, everything might be dry scrub and desert that lay in the scorching heat of the sun, where water was a meagre thing to be scratched for, to be hoarded, drop by precious drop. Down here it was an irritating nuisance, something which made the ground underfoot slippery and treacherous. More than once, the horse slipped and threatened to stumble with him, but always it managed to find its feet. Here and there, patches of the rock were slightly luminous and shone with an eerie greenish sheen.

The air itself was damp and chill and caught at the back of his nostrils as he rode, head lowered where the roof, in places, reached down so low that he was forced to lie on the neck of the horse; and even then, the rough rock scraped at his shoulders. After a while, the metal rails which had been laid to allow the ore-filled carts to be pushed up to the surface, stopped and the horse was splashing through deep pools of water which had gathered over the years. Here, the drainage was simple and crude and most of the moisture was allowed to gather. He was glad when he finally emerged from the mountain, out into the open air and although there was a sickening heat here, among the thorn bushes and heavy yellow sand, it was, temporarily, far better than the claustrophobic dampness of that tunnel.

He put his horse to the gallop now that there was nothing to hinder it, anxious to reach the Morgan ranch before they were expecting him. He knew the workings of Morgan's mind, guessed that with the vigilantes out of town, the other might gather together as many men as he could trust, ride into town, and take it over for himself, building up his strong position there before the vigilantes could get back. If that were the case, then it might suit his plans still further. It could mean that there would be very few men left at the ranch. Morgan would never consider the possibility that there might be danger from that direction.

Sweat poured into his eyes as he rode. Sand, whipped up by the thudding hoofs of his mount, worked its way between his clothing and skin, setting up a terrible itch which was almost unbearable. But he forced himself to ignore it. What he had on his mind was too important for him to stop and make himself comfortable. He had deliberately taken his time coming through the tunnel, but now he would have to make up that time as much as possible. It was too much to expect the vigilantes to overlook the fact that his body was not back there in the canyon and that the Ranger would need proof of his death before he assumed that he had been killed. It was also possible that the Ranger, whoever he was, might be a little more shrewd than he thought and would also head for the Morgan ranch once he had cleared up things back there.

Not that there was any chance of that bunch beating him to the ranch. They would be forced to go back along the Badlands trail and that could take them the best part of the day. He doubted if they could make the Morgan ranch much before nightfall.

He stopped his horse at a muddy waterhole, slid from the saddle and threw himself down in the shade of a spindly cottonwood. The heat of midday lay all around him, lying close to the shimmering face of the desert like a blanket. It threatened to smother him as he lay there, trying to get some of the strength back into his limbs. He drank a few mouthfuls of water from his canteen, washing down the dry, unappetising strips of jerky meat which he had brought with him. The urge to stay there all afternoon, until the lowering sun brought a slight coolness to the desert, was almost more than he could resist. But he fought off the desire, allowed his horse to drink its fill at the waterhole, then climbed back wearily into the saddle. There were still several miles of desert to cross before he hit the main stage trail. After that, the going ought to be a little easier and he reckoned that he ought to reach the ranch just before sundown, an hour or more at least before the vigilantes could make it, even if they rode hard all the way, not stopping to eat on the trail.

His horse plodded on with bowed head after they had been riding for two hours. The heat still lay all around them, shocking up from the ground where the sand seemed to have sucked it out of the air during the morning, only to release it as the sun went down, keeping up the stifling, sickening pressure. His throat felt parched and dry and it was an agony every time he tried to swallow. Now that he was riding north-east, the sun lay behind him, throwing slowly lengthening shadows across the sand, highlighting the narrow rocky gullies which were traps for the unwary rider.

Time and again, sick and stunned by the heat, his head fell forward onto his chest, his eyes lidding and closing with the weariness that flooded over him, making it impossible for him to ride upright in the saddle. The long ride from the canyon was beginning to take its toll of him, but the raging fires of his desire for revenge kept him going. His lips were caked and cracked with the heat and the few sips of water that he allowed himself from the canteen were soaked up instantly by the swollen tongue in his mouth and did not refresh him in the least.

By the time he left the line of rocky buttes behind him and came within sight of the stage trail, the sun was almost touching the line of undulating peaks which were the Diablo Mountains far to the south-west, almost on the border. There was a faint coolness in the air now and shadows were long and dark all about him. Once, he heard the thunder of hoofs in the distance and thought he could make out the cloud of dust raised by the riders, far over on his right, but the heat had affected his vision making it difficult to see properly through the red haze which danced continually in front of his eyes, and he could not be sure.

He crossed the trail and entered the scrub country which lay between it and the borders of Morgan's ranch. Here, he dug his spurs cruelly into the horse's flanks, urging it on to the limit of its waning strength. Now there was a sense of urgency riding him, forcing him on. He was so close to the ranch, so close to the fulfilment of his revenge, that he could scarcely control his anger. As he rode, he kept a sharp lookout for any of the Morgan riders. There might still be a handful out in this part of the spread, herding the beef. But although he saw one large herd grazing on the gentle slopes of the prairie, there was no sign of any hands riding them and he continued on his way, unmolested.

A mile or so further on, he came to the point where Vance had ridden down the boundary wire. He paused for a moment, unsure of what this meant, then gigged the horse and rode through. Everything was still and quiet here and his face tightened into a harsh mask as he rode – parallel with the trail leading up to the ranch. Now, all of the fatigue seemed to have been washed from his body by the wave of fury which lay deep within him, burning at his mind.

As he topped the rise and came within sight of the ranch house, he saw that yellow lights were shining in several of the windows and there was smoke curling up from the chimney. Evidently, someone was still there, even if Morgan himself had headed into town.

Leaving his mount, he went forward on foot in the growing darkness, pulling one of the guns from its holster. He meant to take no chances, even if only Carla Morgan were there. That she-cat would pull a gun on him and cut him down without any compunction if he gave her half a chance. A grim smile passed momentarily over his lips as he edged cautiously forward. Carla and that double-crossing foreman of hers would both be dead before he left this place and headed south for the border and safety in Mexico.

He scouted the place carefully first, and when finally convinced that there were no hands around, watching for intruders, he walked towards the door, kicked it open viciously, and stepped inside. Blinking in the light of the two lamps, he stared about him quickly. Carla Morgan leapt up out of the chair in which she had been sitting and swung to face him. The initial expression of startled surprise gave way instantly to one of cunning.

'What are you doing here, Clem?' she demanded harshly. 'I thought you were to stay back there in the Badlands until I gave the word that it was safe to come out of hiding.'

He smiled wickedly. 'I thought that too, Carla. Seems that someone else had different ideas, though. You wouldn't know who sent that Ranger and those vigilantes out there into the old mine, after me, would you?'

'Vigilantes –? I don't know what you're talking about.'

Hagberg might have been pardoned for mistaking the flush of anger which rose into her beautiful face as one of guilt. His hand tightened on the gun as he stepped forward into the room, gaze swinging swiftly from side to side. 'Where's that double-crossing rat who's in this with you?' he snarled. 'Matt Devlin.'

Carla drew herself up to her full height, meeting his stare without flinching. 'He rode into Big Wheel with my father less than an hour ago,' she answered. 'What do you want with him? He was going to ride out and let you know when it was finished in town and safe for you to come out of hiding. Just what has got into you, Clem? And put that gun away before you do something foolish.'

He kept the gun where it was, a slow, almost lazy smile spreading over his face. 'I should have used this gun on both of you when I had the chance,' he said smoothly.

'You and Devlin were the only ones who knew where my hideout was. Yet that Ranger and the vigilantes he brought with him were able to ride right up to it and take us by surprise this morning at sun-up.'

'If you're suggesting that we gave him that information you're riding the wrong trail, Clem,' she said quickly. 'We want to see him killed just as much as you do. Without your help, this ranch will never be mine until I'm too old to make any use of it. The Doc reckons that my father will live for another twenty years yet, even after getting that bullet in his shoulder.'

'Could be that you figured on letting the vigilantes and my men fight it out back there, hoping that there'd be none left on either side to stand up to you and those men that Devlin has in his pay here on the ranch. I ought to have seen what Devlin had in mind when he started paying them to take orders from him. You didn't need me once you'd got your own force here in opposition to your father.'

'You're wrong, Clem.' The girl had seen something in the outlaw's eyes which told her, better than any words, that he meant to kill her this time. Desperately, she pleaded with him, knowing that someone had informed on him, racking her brain to try to figure out who it might have been. 'If Devlin did it, then I knew nothing about it. I swear that, Clem.'

'You're lying,' he said viciously. 'All the way here, after leaving my men dying back there with vigilante bullets in them, I swore vengeance on you and that coyote of a foreman, and I mean to have it. If he's in town, then I'll go in there and get him even if it means running foul of that Ranger again. Could be I'll take care of your father too at the same time.'

'Then take me with you,' she pleaded. 'I've no love for my father. After what happened the other night when the Ranger shot him in the shoulder, I want to see him killed. This ranch will be mine then and if we work things properly, you could be running it too.'

For a fraction of a second, he lowered the gun, then shook his head. 'I know you too well, Carla,' he said quietly. 'Much too well. I know that you're in love with that foreman and the first chance you got, when my back was turned, one of you would let me have it. Once I've finished what I've set out to do, I'm headed for the Mexican border and nobody is going to get in my way.'

She came closer to him. 'But don't you see. That's exactly what this Ranger wants you to do? He's clever, Clem. I've watched him. He's not like those other three who came. He'll come out on top if we fight like this among ourselves. How do you know that anyone told him where you were hiding out? He could've discovered that for himself. He's been riding out into the Badlands ever since he got here. And he's deliberately playing on your suspicions so that instead of having to fight all of us, he can split us into little groups, fighting each of us in turn. You pride yourself on being a military tactician. You fought for the South in the war. Can't you see what he's doing? Divided, we can't hope to stand against him.'

Hagberg pondered that for a moment, then gave a quick nod, holstering his gun. 'Maybe you're right, Carla. Could be that he found out by himself, or that Devlin told him.' His voice hardened. 'I'm still going to kill that foreman of yours, Carla.'

She smiled up at him. 'Kill him then,' she breathed. 'Then everything in this territory will belong to us. We'll build an empire here, far greater than anything my father planned. There are plenty of men who'll fight with us against the law.'

'We'll need men who can handle guns.'

'We'll get them. Once this is finished and that Ranger is dead, together with those vigilantes. They'll be headed back into town soon. Let them fight it out with my father and the rest of his men. Then we'll go in and pick up the pieces. Nobody will be able to stand against us then.'

He nodded, sank down into one of the chairs in front

of the blazing log fire. 'So this is how you live, Carla,' he said softly, his eyes taking in every detail of the room which had been furnished in the style of the Deep South. Whatever feelings the Northerners may have had about the war, they still appreciated the elegance and tastefully furnished colonial houses. 'I must confess that living out there in the desert for so long, hiding from the law, has made me forget all of the luxuries of life. I feel a little out of place here.'

'You'll soon become used to it again when you own everything here,' she told him. 'When do you intend to ride into town after Matt?'

He shifted his body comfortably in the deep chair. 'Pretty soon,' he said softly. 'That was a mighty long ride across the desert in all that heat. Could you fix something to eat before I go. I need to rest up a little.'

'Just you sit there and I'll fix everything,' she told him. He lay back and watched her go out of the room through slitted eyes. There was a deep weariness in his body and all that he wanted to do was sleep. But he knew that there was still a lot of unfinished business to be attended to before he could rest. Even while he sat there, he was listening to the sounds outside the ranch, the faint sighing murmur of the wind which still blew from the south, ears attentive for the first sound of horsemen riding in that direction. If the Ranger and his friends did come to the ranch, he wanted to be ready for them.

He was so intent on listening for the sound of horses' hoofs, that he failed to notice that the girl had come back, was standing in the open doorway looking across the room at him. When he finally was aware of her presence and turned his head slowly in her direction, he stiffened abruptly as he saw the heavy Winchester rifle which she held in her hands, the barrel covering him as he sat bolt upright in the chair. Carla Morgan laughed throatily, a menacing sound in the stillness.

'You don't think I ever intended you to get away from

here alive, to kill Matt, do you?' she said huskily. 'But I had to throw you off your guard before you pulled that trigger. I'm afraid though that you're not going to get the same chance with me. I'm going to kill you, Clem, then ride out and warn Matt that the Ranger might be headed back towards town, that he's killed all of your men and probably still has plenty of his own men left.'

'Why you conniving—'

Her smile widened as she stepped forward, watching him carefully. 'If you want to go for your guns, Clem, you can always try. I don't want it to be spread around that I shot an unarmed man. But there aren't going to be many people asking questions about you. I'll simply say that you came here at sundown and threatened me, that I was here alone in the ranch and I had to shoot you in self-defence. No jury in the world would convict me on that evidence.'

'You're making a big mistake, Carla,' he said softly, his voice as smooth as the hiss of a snake, almost hypnotic in its quality. 'I said that most of my men had been killed in that gunfight back there, but not all of them. Do you think I would be foolish enough to come riding here alone. After all, I guessed that you were behind this double-cross. We scouted your ranch, and we know that there are none of your men here. But there are three of mine outside with rifles trained on you.'

She laughed thinly. 'I'm not falling for that trick, Hagberg,' she snapped, advancing another step, her dark eyes blazing. 'You were going to kill me when you first came here, even though I knew nothing of what you accused me of. Now it's your turn, and you're going to die right now.'

Deliberately, Hagberg shifted his glance to his right, staring at a point over the girl's shoulder. In spite of herself, involuntarily, she half-turned her head and in that split second presented him with the chance he wanted. Savagely, he leapt upon her, swinging in under the pointing barrel of the rifle, twisting it in her grip. She fought him desperately, tried to throw him off, struggling against him with all of her strength. With an effort, he succeeded in wrenching the gun from her, tried to swing it up, finger fumbling for the trigger, but she hammered at his face with both fists, then used a woman's trick, clawing with her nails at his eyes until he was forced to lose his hold on the rifle and stagger back as blood poured from his forehead and cheeks where her nails had raked across his flesh.

Angrily, cursing under his breath, he struck her a savage blow across the side of the face. She went back against the wall, half falling over the small, polished table. He hit her again, then pulled back his hand swiftly as she bit his arm, sinking her strong white teeth into his flesh. As he pulled himself upright, she snatched at something on the table behind her, bringing her right arm round as she hit him on the side of the head. He uttered a roar of savage anger as the blow half stunned him. Blood from the deep scratches over his eyes almost blinded him so that he seemed to be seeing things through a deep red haze. Backing off, he jerked the gun from its holster and swung on her, realizing in the instant he did so, that she had flung herself forward and downward, grabbing at the rifle where it had fallen on to the floor.

Lowering the gun, he squeezed the trigger, saw her body jerk convulsively, as the bullet hit her in the back. She fell forward on to her face, her outstretched hand falling over the rifle as she hit the floor. Breathing heavily, he holstered the gun, wiping the back of his hand over his face. It came away covered with blood, but he could see a little more clearly now.

Stepping through into the kitchen, he bathed his face under the pump which stood in the corner. The cold water stung fiercely as it touched the cuts on his head, but shocked some of the strength and purpose back into his body and cleared his head. There was a continual thumping at the back of his forehead as the blood pulsed through his veins, but his brain was a little clearer. He knew what he had to do now, ride on into Big Wheel and kill Devlin. Then he would be able to head for the border.

Wiping his face dry, he searched for something with which to bandage his head, finally finding a large red handkerchief in one of the drawers. Swiftly, he tied it around the deep scratches, staunching the blood which still pulsed from them. Clapping his hat on top of his head, he went back into the front room, threw a swift look about him, then turned to leave. It was not until he reached the door that he heard the sudden movement at the back of him. Turning swiftly, his hands snaked for his guns again. But it was too late. Mortally wounded as she was, that shot had not killed Carla Morgan outright as he had supposed. Somehow, she had regained consciousness and managed to lift the heavy rifle, holding it tightly in her hands with the last of her fading strength. Her fingers pressed the trigger just as the last ounce of life left her body. She died before knowing that the bullet had hit Hagberg full in the chest, just below the throat.

He fell backward, slammed against the doorpost by the terrible impact of the slug. A red lance of agony shot through his chest and blackness threatened to engulf him as he leaned there, struggling to remain upright. There was a dull roaring in his ears as he somehow managed to turn and stagger along the short passage and into the cold night air. Several times, he stumbled and fell to his knees during the nightmare journey to where his horse stood at the top of the grassy knoll.

He swayed and clung to the horse, the stench of sweat and sand in his nostrils. He closed his eyes and shook his head, trying to clear it, but that only increased the pain in his chest and brought on the sickening dizziness. He knew that the blood was pouring from just beneath his throat and being soaked up by his shirt, but still insistent, foremost in his mind, was the knowledge that he had to fulfil his mission in Big Wheel. Carla Morgan, in her dying moments, was not going to alter that.

Everything dulled as he tried to pull himself up into the saddle. Several times, he slipped and fell as his nerveless fingers lacked the strength to hold up his body, but finally he made it, slumping over the horse's neck, urging it forward, in the direction of Big Wheel. All of the strength seemed to have drained from his body and it seemed a miracle that he could continue to hang on to the reins as the horse trotted forward through the lush, green grass.

Only once did he think of Carla, lying back there with his bullet in her back, the rifle clutched in her fingers in that last spasm of agony which had laid the mark of death on him, although he did not fully realize it at the moment. But he put the picture out of his mind and tried instead to concentrate on what he had to do when he reached town. But he never reached town. . . .

The lights were still burning yellow in the windows of the Morgan ranch by the time Vance and the rest of the men rode over the low rise and then put their horses to the gallop. There was no sign apart from the lights that the place was still occupied, but Vance was taking no chances. His keen-eyed gaze told him that the front door was wide open, but he could see no sign of any horses tethered there in front of the house.

'If you're in there, Morgan, you'd better come out here with your hands raised. That goes for your daughter and Devlin too.' He shouted the words loudly as he reined his horse twenty yards or so from the ranch.

He waited for two minutes, then turned to Doc Manton. 'There's something wrong here, Doc,' he said tightly. 'I reckon I'll go down there and take a look. You stay here with the others. If it is a trap and I don't come back, then start shooting. You understand?'

'Sure you don't want me to come down there with you?' asked the other. 'It has all the looks of a trap from here.'

'Nope. I'll be all right by myself. Just remain here and be sure that the others know exactly what to do.'

'Fair enough. You know what you're doing.' Vance

thought he detected a faint note of relief in the other's tone, but he disregarded it, set spurs to his mount and rode down into the courtyard in front of the ranch. Silently, he slipped from the saddle, jerked one of the guns from its holster, and strode in towards the open door. As he approached, he could see that the short corridor which lay beyond it was empty. There was still the feeling in his mind that the place was not quite as deserted as it seemed. Lowering his head, he went inside, reached the end of the corridor, then stepped through into the front room. Then he holstered his gun, turned Carla Morgan over gently, and noticed the bullet wound in her back, just between the shoulder blades. She had been dead for almost an hour, he estimated, then made a quick check of the other rooms. Apart from the body of the dead girl, the ranch was empty.

He went to the door and signalled the others to come in. Doc Manton led the way. He glanced swiftly at Vance as he saw the girl lying on the floor then went down on one knee beside her.

'I didn't kill her if that's what you're wondering,' said Vance slowly. 'She was lying there when I came in. It ain't difficult to figure out what must have happened. Hagberg did come here, seeking vengeance. Probably thought that she was the one who gave us the information about his hideout. He must have shot her from somewhere close at hand. Looks as though there's been a struggle here too. She sold her life dearly.'

'Probably more dearly than she realized,' said one of the men enigmatically. He picked up the rifle which had been lying beneath the girl's body and sniffed the barrel experimentally. 'This has been fired and recently. She may have hit him too. Could be that—'

He broke off as another of the men gave a sudden shout and pointed to the door of the room. 'There's blood here, on the post and on the floor. If it was Hagberg, I'd say he was pretty badly hurt. He was bleeding a lot when he left here. Where'd you figure he'd be headed, Vance?'

'Could be that he's riding for Big Wheel. Since there's no sign here of Devlin, I reckon that's where he must've gone. But with a wound like that, I'd say he couldn't have gone very far. Reckon once we've made a good search of this place, we'll ride in that direction and take a good look. We may find him somewhere along the trail.'

They made a thorough search of the ranch and in one of the desks in the room at the back, which was obviously the one that Morgan used himself, they found papers and documents, land grants and bills of sale which proved conclusively that much of the land which Morgan owned, together with many of the saloons in Big Wheel, had been obtained illegally, many at revolver point.

Doc Manton studied them minutely in the light of the lamp on the table. When he finally looked up, he said quietly, 'Reckon there's enough evidence here to hang Morgan three times over. There'll be a lot of folk in Big Wheel who'll be mighty grateful to you, Ranger, in a lot of ways for what you've done. We'll be able to see to it that they get their land back and cattle. Some of these papers point to rustling by Morgan's men, brand changing, and the like. They'll sure stand up in a court of law.'

'Reckon you'll have to elect yourselves a new sheriff first,' suggested Vance quietly. He handed a sheaf of papers back to Manton. 'But first, we have to deal with Morgan. No use in making any plans for the future if we can't finish him in the same way that we finished Hagberg and his outlaws.'

'Guess you're right,' said the other soberly. He thrust the papers into the voluminous pockets of his black coat. 'There's still work to be done tonight. Mebbe by tomorrow, this whole territory is going to be a better place.'

They went out, leaving Carla Morgan's body in the large, well-furnished room, and saddled up. One of the men suggested putting a torch to the ranch, but both Vance and Doc Manton refused to hear of this.

A mile along the trail, they came upon a riderless horse standing among a clump of trees. One of the men brought it in, gave it a quick glance. 'Could be the one that Hagberg was riding,' he said hoarsely. 'There's yellow sand on its flanks and under the saddle. Been ridden pretty hard too sometime during the day.'

'If it is, then I reckon that Hagberg must be somewhere close by,' said Vance. 'He can't have gone far on foot, particularly if he's been badly wounded.'

The men scattered and began searching, finally finding Hagberg's body among a small cluster of rocks where he had somehow dragged himself after falling out of the saddle. Vance stood looking down at him, dispassionately. The outlaw leader was dead and it was clear that Carla Morgan had been instrumental in killing him. Perhaps it was poetic justice, he thought, as he went back to his horse. When thieves and killers fell out, their reign of terror soon ended.

Several of the men threw sidelong glances at the body as they rode by and Vance knew what they were thinking. Had they not decided to take matters in their own hands, this man might still be alive, might still be able to ride into Big Wheel whenever he pleased, stealing and plundering, while the entire population fled in fear and terror into the countryside, coming out of their holes like rats once he had ridden back into the hills again.

If only the decent people would realize that they outnumbered these outlaws and killers everywhere in the state and banded themselves together to deal with these men, it would not be long before law and order were restored to the frontier territories. But too often, the townsfolk, the nesters and the straight cattlemen were afraid; and it was on fear that these gunslingers founded their empires.

7
Outlaws in Town

Big Wheel lay in front of them at the end of their long ride from the Morgan spread. They rode slowly, well strung out, knowing that Morgan was here with the whole bunch of his men and that the cattle boss would have had no difficulty in persuading his men to stick together now, especially after he must have known that Vance was returning with most of the vigilantes. To the ranchers from the Morgan spread, this could mean only one thing. That Hagberg and his outlaws had been utterly wiped out and they could expect no assistance from them. It also meant that those men who had thrown in their lot with Devlin, unknown to Morgan, would also have to stand and fight with the rest now that there was no chance of going over to join the outlaws.

Vance figured that there would be the best of fifty men in town, holed up somewhere, ready to fight it out with them. How many more of the townsfolk would join them after the fighting started was something he did not know. They sorely needed more men who could handle guns if they were to drive these critters out of Big Wheel for good. He threw swift, sideways glances at the men who rode with him along the stage trail which led into town. They rode silently, grim-faced and tall in the saddle. Most of them had wives and families in the town and were probably wondering how many of them would still be alive now that Morgan and his men were in command.

The question of hostages having been taken was uppermost in Vance's mind, but he did not voice his fears. Once a man knew that his wife and children were being held by these men as a safeguard for their own welfare, he could scarcely be blamed if he threw in his hand and refused to fight.

In the lead, with Doc Manton a little distance behind him, on one side, Vance led the way into Big Wheel. The streets were empty. No horses were tied to the hitching posts outside the saloons. In front of them, the main street was ominously quiet and deserted. Lights still shone in most of the windows, but they only served to accentuate the stillness and emptiness. The sound of their hoofs seemed oddly loud in the clinging silence as they rode forward very slowly, eyes alert, covering every building on the way.

They had almost drawn level with the livery stables when Devlin's voice yelled from one of the windows of the Golden Nugget saloon: 'Here we are, Ranger. This is as far as you and those yeller-livered vigilantes at the back of you go. If you know what's good for you, turn round and ride out of town – and don't come back. We've taken over here.'

'What has Morgan got to say to that speech?' called Vance, halting his horse.

'He agrees with it,' shouted the other harshly. 'Now turn around and git!'

'Why don't he speak for himself?' Vance eased himself up in the saddle, hands hovering close to the guns at his waist. 'Could it be that he ain't in any fit condition to talk to us? Seems you've taken on a lot for yourself, Devlin. I've had quite an interesting talk with a friend of yours. Clem

Hagberg. He told me quite a lot about the plans you'd made together, to get Morgan's ranch from him, by marrying Carla. Trouble is that it won't happen now.'

'You don't know what you're talking about, Ranger,' snarled the other.

'No? Could be that you don't know that Carla is dead – Hagberg too.'

For a moment, there was a tight pause, then the other's voice, not quite as sure of itself now, yelled: 'You're lying, Ranger. When we've finished with you, mebbe I'll take a ride over for a look-see myself.'

Vance pressed home his advantage. While he had been holding the other in conversation, his men had been spreading themselves out along both sides of the street, moving slowly forward, rifles ready. It seemed likely that Devlin had not missed a trick and had some men in the building on the opposite side of the street to the Golden Nugget, just in case they tried to rush the saloon.

'We found Carla dead at the ranch, Devlin. Hagberg had shot her. Seems they must've quarrelled about something important. But she got him with a rifle before she died. We found his body near the boundary of the spread. Reckon he must've been headed this way with something burning him up, if he travelled with that wound in his chest. Could it have been that he was coming to kill you, Devlin? There ain't many things that will force a man to go to his death like that, when he could have been clear across the Mexican border by now.'

'Damn you, Ranger, you talk too much!' The other's hard voice was punctuated by a gunshot and a bullet ploughed a neat furrow through the wooden wall close to Vance's head. He threw himself sideways out of the saddle in a single, smooth motion, landed lightly on his feet and came up again, his gun in his hand, spitting lead at the windows of the saloon.

Gunfire broke out in that instant as the outlaws returned the fire. Glass shattered and tinkled on to the boardwalks. As Vance had suspected, some of the fire was coming from the building next to the livery stables, where more of the ranch-hands had been in hiding. Rifle-fire poured into them from the vigilantes, crouched down behind the water troughs and at the back of the tall barrels which stood on the boardwalks in front of one of the other saloons.

Wriggling his way forward, Vance came up behind one of the barrels and emptied his gun at one of the windows of the saloon. He had the satisfaction of seeing one of the men, a dark shadow silhouetted against the glare of light from inside the building, suddenly throw up his arms and fall back into the room as the bullet found its mark.

More slugs hammered into the wood of the barrel as he ducked back, away from the return fire. These men would be difficult to dislodge from that place, he decided. As a defensive position, it was an excellent place from which to conduct a pitched battle. No doubt Morgan himself had chosen it with an eye to defence. He doubted if Devlin would possess any of the older man's military training.

Swiftly, he cast about him for some way of getting inside without being seen. Once in the building, he would be able to take them by surprise, from behind. But it was not going to be easy. Morgan, or Devlin, would have foreseen anything like that and the rear of the building was as likely to be watched as the front. But there was no time to be lost if he was to prevent a wholesale slaughter out here in the main street. Already, several of the men who had ridden with him had been hit while he doubted whether more than half a dozen of the enemy had been killed or badly wounded.

He turned to the man crouching down beside him. 'I'm going to try to get into the saloon from the rear,' he said tightly. 'Keep pumping slugs into them from here until I get inside.'

'You don't stand much chance of that,' declared the other swiftly. 'They'll have men watching that way in too.'

'I know. But that's a risk I'll have to take. If we keep firing from here they'll have the edge on us all of the time. I've got to find some way in.'

'Want me to come with you?' prompted the other, pushing himself slowly to his feet. 'Four guns are better than two in a fight like this.'

Vance nodded as he reached a sudden decision. It might mean that they stood only half the chance of getting through unseen, but if there were many men at the back of the saloon, this man might be able to hold them off while he got inside.

The two of them skirted the side of the street, darted down the narrow alley which led between tall walls stretching up into the night. The sound of gunfire still crashed out behind them in the street and there was the occasional whine of tortured metal as a ricochet flew through the night, or the scream of a wounded man as a slug found its mark. They reached the corner of the building, stood quite still for a moment, searching with eyes and ears.

'They don't seem to have this side guarded,' whispered the man beside him.

Vance shook his head. 'They'll have a handful of men here. Morgan wouldn't be such a fool as to leave his rear unguarded.'

They slipped forward into the darkness. Breaking cover, Vance darted forward until he was less than twenty feet from the back of the saloon. In that same moment, his eye saw the orange muzzle flash as a gun spat flame. He went down instantly, trained reflexes hurling him to the ground. The slug spent itself harmlessly, whining over his head like an angry hornet. But he had been seen. He lunged forward again, a fleet shadow in the darkness. Another shot rang out, but this time, it came from behind him. He reached the wall and crouched close against it, pressing his body well in to the stonework, knowing that so long as he was there, it would be practically impossible for any gunman to hit him without exposing himself to his return fire.

For a moment, he glimpsed the man's head as it showed briefly at the back of the window. The guns in his hands spoke sharply, slamming against his wrists. The head jerked back with a loud, despairing cry and taking his life in his hands, Vance ran along the rear of the building towards the window where the man had appeared so briefly. Reaching it, he swung himself inside the room beyond. For all he knew that cry could have been a ruse to get him out into the open, the man he had shot at could be standing there in the dimness with his sixes trained on the window, ready to press the triggers the instant he appeared. Or he could, at that very moment, be running through the building to warn Devlin of what was happening.

Fortunately, he was doing neither. As he stepped into the room Vance stumbled over his body, lying inertly at the back of the window. He felt the other's pulse quickly, made certain that he was dead, then went back to the window and uttered a low whistle. The other man joined him in a few moments and Vance helped him inside.

'Follow me,' he hissed thinly, 'and no noise, if you value your life.'

The other nodded to show that he understood and followed close on Vance's heels. They went through the half-open door and found themselves in a long corridor, with more doors opening off from it on both sides.

As they reached the end of it, they almost bumped into a man coming quickly down the stairs. Their sudden appearance had taken the gunman completely by surprise. He had obviously never taken into consideration that anyone could get in past the guards at the windows. This unexpected move caught him utterly off balance. He tried to go for his sixes, to bring them to bear on Vance, swinging them up in a blur of movement, squeezing the triggers in the same moment. The guns roared and the slugs blasted themselves into the wooden floor around Vance's feet as he fired himself. The man's lips were drawn back into a cruel grin of almost wolfish pleasure. But the expression changed swiftly to one of utter amazement as the red stain appeared on his shirt and he toppled forward with a tired sigh as his last breath escaped from his lungs. His guns dropped to the floor with a loud clatter as he slumped at Vance's feet.

'Quickly!' urged Vance to the other. 'They may have heard that shooting. If they come to investigate, we'll have to shoot our way through.'

He led the way up the stairs, knowing that to go through into the bar on the ground floor would give them no advantage and would expose them to a concentrated fire without giving them any additional cover. From upstairs, they could fire down at the men below and create more havoc before they were seen. The din of gunfire met them as they reached the top of the stairs and ran along the corridor in front of them. Any noise that their boots may have made was drowned completely in the rattle of Colts and Winchesters.

Vance reached the low rail which overlooked the downstairs bar and peered over. There were close on thirty men down there, he estimated, taking in everything in a single, well-trained glance. The others would be across the street in the other building. Morgan had deployed his forces well and was in an exceptional position. No doubt he had made certain that they had plenty of ammunition and sufficient food and water to withstand a long siege if necessary.

Nodding to the man beside him to take up his position a little further along the rail, he started firing, picking his targets carefully, making every slug count. Five men dropped, falling away from the windows, and still no one had turned to return their fire. Then it dawned on him. The sound of their own fire was mingling with the din down there and it was almost impossible for anyone there to realize that these men were being shot in the back. He sighted on a man leaning against one of the windows, fired a couple of shots and saw the other drop his rifle and slump tiredly on to the floor. But in that moment, he must have exposed himself, for a hoarse voice from somewhere below him yelled: 'Two of them. Up there on the top floor.'

Several men turned and began firing at them. Ducking back behind the thick wooden post, Vance heard the bullets sing their vicious hum of death as they hit the wooden beams close by. Swiftly, he twisted himself sideways and flung himself down on to the floor as more guns blasted from down below. The gunmen down there were now shooting at a grave disadvantage. They were still completely exposed to his fire, whereas it was possible for him to shoot at them without exposing too much of his body.

From outside, he heard the savage roar of gunfire as the vigilantes stepped up their attack on the saloon. Whether or not they realized that, somehow, he had got inside and was attacking from the rear, he did not know. But they seemed to have swung around the building so as to be attacking it from all sides. Pulling himself upright, exposing himself for several seconds, he emptied his guns into the men below. Several of them were hit before they could scramble under cover, behind the upturned tables which had been flung up to meet this new, and unexpected, attack from behind.

He turned to yell a word of encouragement to his companion, then stopped short. The man lay half over the balcony, with his arms hanging limp. Even as he went forward, crouching down low on one knee, he knew that there was nothing he could do for the man. The bullet had hit him in the chest, killing him instantly, pitching him forward, his gun dropping from nerveless fingers into the saloon beneath.

Going back under cover, Vance thrust shells into his guns. He had little ammunition left now, and hoped that the men outside would soon rush the place.

He had no way of telling how things were progressing in that other building directly across the street, but here the men below were so utterly demoralized by this attack from the rear, that one good, concerted attack on the building ought to be enough to carry the day. He narrowed his eyes as he glimpsed a familiar figure down below. Devlin had spotted him and was moving cautiously forward, scuttling crablike from one overturned table to another, never showing himself for more than a second at a time. He had a gun in his right hand and there was a mask of deadly intent on his face. Vance aimed a snap shot at the foreman as he ran across an open space, but the bullet missed, ploughed into the woodwork of the floor and a moment later, the man had vanished out of sight beneath him, yelling something to the men close at hand as he ran past them.

A sudden volley of fire from below hammered around Vance as he crouched back. Now he knew what the foreman's order had been. To keep him covered from below while the other had a chance to make it up those stairs and take him from behind. He sucked in a deep breath and steadied himself against the rail. It was possible that a stray ricochet from below might hit him, but a direct shot stood little chance so long as he remained where he was. But he could not stay there for long, not with that vicious killer stalking up the stairs, intent on slaying him.

Drawing in a deep breath, he edged his way forward an inch at a time. A slug laid a red-hot brand along his arm. He knew the coldly, calculating way in which the foreman would make his attack. Whether or not the other had believed him when he had said that Carla Morgan and Hagberg were dead, it would make no difference to the fact that he intended to kill Vance. If he was to stay alive and still take over the Morgan spread, whether or not he killed Morgan himself, or was trusting on that to happen tonight, he had to kill the Ranger.

An inch at a time, Vance eased himself away from the

edge of the balcony, and over to the door which opened out on to the wide corridor along which Devlin would have to come if he was to reach him. He was almost at the door when he heard the other reach the top of the stairs and start forward along the corridor. Throwing caution to the winds, Vance stepped out in full view of the other and threw two shots along the corridor at the dimly seen figure at the far end. Devlin hurled himself sideways, crashing into one of the doors, knocking it open and slipping into the room.

From the front of the saloon, the roar of sixes still slammed on the air, but the fire from inside the building was slowly dying down. Too many of the men down there had been killed or wounded when he and his companion had burst upon them from the balcony. That had been the turning point and the men outside, under Doc Manton, seemed to sense that something had happened, that this was not just another trick to lure them forward.

Dimly, a moment later, he was aware of a harsh yelling, the crashing of glass and doors as the vigilantes came pouring into the saloon from the street, firing as they advanced. Devlin must have heard the sound too and realized what it portended, for he gave a snarl of rage and fired swiftly along the corridor as Vance hurled himself back under cover. The bullets nicked his shoulder but did not draw blood and he cursed himself for his stupidity.

'This is where you get it, Vance,' snarled the other harshly, his voice reaching the Ranger clearly, although he kept himself out of sight. 'You tried to make me look a fool in front of Carla that day in the hotel and I never forgive a man who does that. He has to die. And you will die very soon, I promise you.'

'You don't stand a chance,' said Vance smoothly. 'You'll never get out of this place alive. You'll swing out there with Morgan and any others these people take alive. You've ridden roughshod over them too long, now they've turned against you and this time, it will be you who'll end up on the rope.'

'Mebbe so. But you'll never live to see that happen, Vance. I've been waiting for this chance a long time, to meet you face to face on level terms, to shoot you down.'

'Seems to me that you're doing a mighty lot of talking and no action,' said Vance softly, deliberately trying to goad the other into making his move. 'No sense in hiding in that room, is there? Step out and let's get it over with.'

There was a low, evil chuckle. 'If you're trying to taunt me out into the open, Vance, you're wasting your breath. Could be that you're faster than me. According to the stories I've heard, you're pretty good on the draw, killed quite a few men back there in Dodge. But I don't aim to give you the chance to shoot me down like you did those others with Hagberg.'

'No? What you figure on doing? Getting me to turn round so that you can shoot me in the back? I don't know whether it was you or Hagberg who killed those three Rangers. Hagberg's dead so that's my part of the bargain settled. I didn't aim to have to fight it out with you when I first came into Big Wheel, but it seems there are more killers here than I'd figured.'

'Now who's doing all the talking,' hissed the other.

Vance narrowed his eyes and steadied himself at the end of the corridor, confident from the sound of the other's voice that he intended to make his play very soon, just as soon as he figured he had lulled Vance into a state of false security. There had been something oddly hypnotic about the other's voice and he knew that the other had spoken like that deliberately in an attempt to throw him off his guard.

When Devlin moved, the attack came with the swiftness and unexpectedness of a striking rattler. He threw himself swiftly out into the open, stood there in the middle of the corridor blazing away with both sixes. Vance dropped swiftly on to one knee, bringing up his own guns in a blur of motion. He felt the whiplash of bullets striking the air close to his head. The instinctive motion had saved his life.

But it had jarred his aim and his bullets missed the other as Devlin darted into another, nearer room on the other side of the corridor.

There was silence in the corridor as he stood there with his back against the side of the door, every sense stretched almost to breaking point by the tension. He imagined that he could hear the other man breathing harshly in the shadows at the side of the passage. When Devlin made his move again, it would be his last chance to kill him. He had no more bullets left in his belt, only those that were still in the chambers of his guns.

He was debating the wisdom of carrying the attack to the other, taking him by surprise, when the foreman moved. He swung himself sharply around the side of the door, both guns hammering in his hands. Something scorched past Vance's cheek as he fired back. He thought he had hit the other in the moment that Devlin had shown himself. Then there came two dull, ominous clicks as the hammers of his guns hit empty chambers.

Devlin must have heard the sound too, for he suddenly stepped out into the middle of the corridor, both guns held in his hands. He could see the malevolent look in the foreman's eyes and thought this is surely the finish. Nothing could stop that killer from squeezing the triggers of his guns and cutting him down where he stood. He braced himself for the smashing impact of the bullets, the useless guns in his hands. The seconds seemed to drag themselves by as individual eternities. The other's knuckles gleamed white with the pressure he was exerting. Then he pressed the triggers. A second fled before Vance realized that the million-to-one chance had happened, that both of the other's guns were also empty. But he had only a second or so to allow the realization of that to enter his mind, before the other flung himself forward with a savage curse, dropping one of the guns and using the other as a club.

Turning his head instinctively, he could only duck sufficiently beneath that blow so that the hard metal glanced off his shoulder, numbing his right arm. The gun dropped from fingers suddenly nerveless as the shock of that blow travelled down his arm and into his hand. He tried to use his left hand, to use the gun which he still held in it, but the other swung his arm, striking him savagely on the wrist so that he was forced to release his hold on his only weapon. It flew from his fingers and clattered to the floor somewhere along the corridor.

Now it was to be a fight to the finish with no quarter asked and none given. He guessed that the other would be a dirty fighter, would use every means possible to kill him. The foreman's face contorted and flamed with anger. He brought up his right foot swiftly. It caught Vance on the side of the leg, throwing him off balance. He came up hard against the wall of the corridor, twisted in mid air and landed on his feet as the other dived in. Shifting sideways, he felt the blow of the other's body striking him at an angle. Devlin's breath, rasping in his throat, told him that the other was out of training, but he felt the other's clutching arms as the foreman caught hold of him and tried desperately to hang on to him, to drag him down to the floor where he could use his superior weight to hold him there. Swiftly, putting everything behind it, Vance brought over his left fist, knuckles bunched into a hard ball. It caught the other on the cheek and drew blood, scraping downwards to his chin. The foreman reeled back under the impact of that blow and fell on to his side. With an effort, Vance got to his feet and stood there, swaying slightly, his right shoulder still numb where the other had crashed into it. There was a vague blurring in front of his eyes and a dull throbbing at the back of his temples. But a moment later, there was no time to realize any of this for the other had thrust himself upright and bellowing like an angry bull, came charging in, arms spread wide, a murderous glint in his eyes.

Vance tried to step to one side to avoid the other's mad

rush, but found himself hard up against the wall. The other threw his arms swiftly about Vance's middle and pulled him close, hugging him tightly in a bear-hug that was designed to snap the lawman's back like a rotten twig. Grimly, he held on as the corridor started to spin around him. Desperately, he let in a right and a left to the other man's chin, but it was impossible to put any real weight behind the blows and Devlin merely grinned, thinning his lips back across his teeth in an animal-like snarl of defiance, increasing the pressure on Vance's back.

Fighting savagely to suck air into his heaving lungs, he hammered away at the other's face with his clenched fists, but the other merely lowered his head and thrust it hard against his cheek.

There were going to be no ethics to this fight, Vance decided. The other meant to kill him. Swiftly, he changed his tactics, stamping down as hard as he could on to the top of the other's right foot. The foreman gave a yelp of angry pain and relaxed his grip a little. Vance drew in a quick breath which cleared his head a little and allowed some of the strength to flow back into his body. The corridor and walls no longer danced and swayed in front of his vision. Striking viciously at the other's head, he suddenly relaxed the muscles of his legs completely, allowing himself to fall back, bringing all of his deadweight to bear on the foreman's arms. Caught off balance, the other staggered forward, desperately trying to regain his balance. As he struggled to keep on his feet, Vance thrust out his arms to their full length and struck savagely at the back of the other's lowered neck. Devlin uttered a low grunt and fell forward, his legs turning to putty and his arms opening a little.

Now that he could breathe more easily, Vance brought up his knee and hit the other in the pit of the stomach, driving all of the wind out of his body. Devlin fell back, reeling against the wall, his mouth hanging slackly open as he tried to draw air down into his lungs. Vance hit him again for good measure across the adam's apple and he dropped on to his knees, face twisted as he gasped for breath.

There was little fight left in the other now. He lay against the wall, staring up at Vance through angry, pain-filled eyes, only making a half-conscious groaning sound. His lips moved convulsively but no words came out.

'Reckon you've had enough, Devlin ' said Vance tightly, forcing evenness into his voice. 'I'll see that you're taken into custody and tried. There'll be plenty of charges brought against you and I've little doubt that the jury will find you guilty of them all, particularly since they won't be afraid to bring in a proper verdict this time. You'll find the Sheriff in jail alongside you. There'll be a rope waiting for most of you when this is finished.'

He glanced up, at the sudden sound on the stairs. A bunch of men came into sight, stopped as they caught sight of him, then walked forward quickly. Doc Manton was with them. They stood staring down at the semi-conscious figure of Matt Devlin for a moment, then Manton turned to Vance.

'I see you managed to catch up with him and take him alive for trial.'

'That's right. He tried to kill me twice, once with his guns and then with his fists. Reckon you'd better take him down and lock him up in jail. How's it going down there?'

'Just fine, Vance, just fine. Most of 'em have surren-dered. When they saw that they never had no chance, they threw down their guns and came along with their hands over their heads. Only sensible thing to do, of course.'

'And Morgan? What happened to him?'

'He's down there right now,' declared Manton. 'Had to take a look at him myself before they took him away. He'd been shot in the shoulder from pretty close range and the slug was still in the wound. Had the devil's own job prob-ing for it until I got it out.'

'My shot hit him in the shoulder a couple of nights ago,' said Vance, puzzled. 'Y'mean that his daughter and Devlin here left him all that time with a slug in his shoulder and then brung him out here just for a show of strength.'

'Could be, Vance. He wasn't more than half-conscious when I got to him. Didn't seem to know where he was most of the time. Could be that the rest of the men would only obey him and wouldn't take any of their orders from Devlin. And he'd need every man he could get here.'

'Reckon I must have underestimated this man when I first came here,' mused Vance, staring down at the other. He rubbed his shoulder where the circulation was just coming back. 'I figured him for a cheap gunslammer, but he seems to have been one of the brains behind everything that's happened.'

'Mebbe so,' grunted one of the men, straightening up, 'but I reckon he'll be making no more trouble from now on.'

Vance nodded and left the small group at the top of the stairs, going down into the saloon below. The gunfight had been savage while it had lasted and over half of the Morgan ranch-hands had been killed. Now that the fighting had finished, several of the townsfolk had come in and were tidying up the tables which had been overturned and the glasses that had been smashed. Vance noticed several of the women among them.

Near the door, he found Morgan. The one-time cattle boss was supported by two of the vigilantes. He hung between them like a badly injured man, his face grey. When he lifted his head, it was clear that he recognized Vance straight away for his lips curled back over his teeth and he said softly, haltingly: 'I always figured there'd come a time when we got one too many Rangers riding into Big Wheel, trying to find out what happened to the others. I said that from the beginning, but neither Carla nor Hagberg would listen to me. They were so sure that they could run this territory between them that they never bothered to heed any of my advice. I hope they're glad at what has happened.'

'You've quite a lot to answer for yourself,' Vance told him tightly. 'We came across some very important papers and documents in the drawer in your study. They told us quite a lot of things we didn't know before. Even if they aren't enough to hang you, I reckon you can resign yourself to spending most of your life in jail.'

'Where's Devlin? Is that coyote dead?' Something approaching bitterness touched the old man's voice.

'They're bringing him down now,' Vance told him pointing in the direction of the wide stairway where three men were bringing Devlin down. The foreman seemed to have recovered from the blow on the throat and walked upright, staring straight in front of him. He strode past Morgan without a single, sideways look, almost as if unaware of his presence.

'He'll hang for his deeds,' Vance promised the other. 'We've got enough on him for that. As for you, I reckon you're completely finished. Your daughter is dead back there at the ranch and Hagberg too. It's ironic, isn't it, how swiftly the empire you've built up over the years, one grown on fraud and murder, can come toppling down about your ears in as many minutes.'

The other shrugged and turned away. A moment later, they had taken him out of the saloon and were helping him across to the sheriff's office. Here, a few moments later, Vance found the portly sheriff vainly protesting his innocence to the other vigilantes. He glanced round swiftly as Vance strode into the office.

'You'll testify to the fact that I wasn't in Morgan's pay, won't you?' he pleaded. 'I simply had to carry out Morgan's orders, otherwise he threatened to shoot me. Besides, I was the only one in town you confided in when you first arrived. You told me then that you were a Ranger. And I never betrayed that confidence, did I?'

'Didn't you?' said Vance thinly, ominously. 'Someone did, because Morgan knew all about it within a few hours of my arrival here. And as you say, you were the only one in town in whom I confided.'

'But I would never have – I mean it was impossible for me to have—'

'Better save your breath,' said Vance wearily. He turned to Doc Manton. 'I reckon you'd better lock him up with the others. The circuit judge can decide the fit punishment for a crooked lawman when he gets here. I'm pretty certain myself what the sentence will be.'

The other made as if to continue with his protests, then obviously thought better of it and sullenly followed Doc Manton along the narrow corridor to the cells at the rear of the building, the cells where Vance himself had spent some time, waiting for the lynching mob.

Doc Manton came back with the large bunch of keys and hung them up on the hook beside the desk. He glanced across at Vance. 'We'll elect a new Sheriff as soon as we can, Vance,' he said quietly. 'In the meantime, we'll need someone here to keep the peace for a few days while the town settles down. This is the biggest thing that has happened to Big Wheel since it was founded.'

'I'll stick around until you get yourselves a new Sheriff,' said Vance, nodding, 'provided that it isn't too long. But after what's happened today, I figure this calls for a drink. I wonder if they've managed to clean the Golden Nugget up yet so that decent citizens can get a cold beer.'

'I reckon they might have,' answered the other. From outside, there came the sound of men on horseback riding into town. But from now on, thought Vance inwardly, the people here would not have to fear the sound of horses' hoofs in the street. The outlaws had been killed and those who were still alive were where they belonged, in jail.

Doc Manton led the way to the saloon, held open the door for Vance to step through. Vance looked about him in astonishment. It seemed incredible that in so short a space of time, such a transformation could have taken place. All of the polished tables were back in position. A couple of white-aproned bartenders were behind the bar and Vance recognized one of them as a man who had accompanied them into the Badlands when they had rounded up the Hagberg gang.

'Everything is on the house tonight,' said the bartender, as he pulled out his money. Smiling, he put it back into his pocket and picked up his drink. In one corner of the room, a blonde-haired woman was standing by the old upright piano while a bowler-hatted man played it inexpertly, but tunefully enough for the melody to be recognized. A small group were clustered around one of the tables playing Faro. In other words, thought Vance, everything was swiftly getting back to normal. In the years to come, it would need a good Sheriff here to make sure that no one else ever tried to set himself up around these parts. There was always that danger that someone would come along, some lawless elements from the east, seeking a soft spot where they could move in and take over.

But he had the idea that these people had seen now what could be done provided that they banded together in the face of danger and met it as one. If they put their fears behind them and went out determined to wipe out any outlaws who tried to take over the town.

Big Wheel had learned its lesson and he hoped inwardly that it would remember it. As for himself, he had done his job and had avenged the deaths of those three Rangers who had ridden into this town long before, seeking to bring law and order with them. They had not been as fortunate as he was, but he had the feeling that none of them had died in vain. The Hagberg gang was no more. Morgan and his daughter, and Matt Devlin were finished, one way or another.

He finished his drink and went out through the batwing doors, standing for a moment in the street. The

stars were out in their thousands over his head and somewhere down the street a horse sneezed the dust of the trail
out of its nostrils and stomped the earth impatiently.